"You're not  this, are yo

I sighed. Bill knew me too well. "I've never been a big fan of Christmas, not even as a kid."

"That's hard to believe. What kid doesn't like Christmas?"

"My mother always hijacked the holiday."

"Your family didn't celebrate?"

"We celebrated all right, in my family's own inimitable way."

Bill pulled me toward him and tipped my chin with his finger until our eyes met. "You don't have to do this—" he nodded toward the box with my Mrs. Claus costume "—if you don't want to."

I hesitated. Part of me wanted to take the out he'd given me and run.

"You've been telling me I need to lighten up and have some fun. So I'll give it my best shot," I said, determined to enjoy myself.

Even if it killed me.

Charlotte Douglas

USA TODAY bestselling author Charlotte Douglas, a versatile writer who has produced over twenty-five books, including romances, suspense, gothics and even a *Star Trek* novel, has now created a mystery series featuring Maggie Skerritt, a witty and irreverent homicide detective in a small fictional town on Florida's central west coast.

Douglas's life has been as varied as her writings. Born in North Carolina and raised in Florida, she earned her degree in English from the University of North Carolina at Chapel Hill and attended graduate school at the University of South Florida in Tampa. She has worked as an actor, a journalist and a church musician and taught English and speech at the secondary and college level for almost two decades. For several summers while newly married and still in college, she even manned a U.S. Forest Service lookout in northwest Montana with her husband.

Married to her high school sweetheart for over four decades, Douglas now writes full-time. With her husband and their two cairn terriers, she divides her year between their home on Florida's central west coast—a place not unlike Pelican Bay—and their mountaintop retreat in the Great Smokies of North Carolina.

She enjoys hearing from readers, who can contact her at charlottedouglas1@juno.com.

CHARLOTTE DOUGLAS
HOLIDAYS ARE MURDER

HOLIDAYS ARE MURDER

copyright © 2005 Charlotte Douglas

isbn 0373230516

This edition published by arrangement with Harlequin Books S.A.

® and TM are trademarks of the publisher. Trademarks indicated with
® are registered in the United States Patent and Trademark Office, the
Canadian Trade Marks Office and in other countries.

TheNextNovel.com

 HARLEQUIN®

PRINTED IN U.S.A.

Dear Reader,

Christmas in west central Florida isn't exactly a Currier and Ives event. We still celebrate with family and friends, but we make our snow angels in white sugar sand instead of the frozen white stuff. Poinsettias grow in the landscape as well as sprouting in pots in the produce aisle and at the florist's. And we've been known to crank up the air-conditioning in order to roast our chestnuts on an open fire. Floridians, as Bill Malcolm will show you, adapt creatively to Yuletide celebrations in the land of palm trees, sunshine and surf.

Like many of us, Maggie Skerritt has a lot on her plate for the holidays. I hope you'll enjoy her at her best—and worst—in *Holidays Are Murder*, and that you'll return to Pelican Bay in March 2006 for *Spring Break*, when Maggie matches wits with murderers again.

Happy reading, and happy holidays!

Charlotte Douglas

CHAPTER I

The phone rang at 12:30 a.m., awakening me from a deep sleep.

"Give me a break, Darcy," I complained to the night dispatcher who'd called. "I'm still on vacation."

"Sorry, Maggie. According to the chief, you're back on the clock as of midnight."

George Shelton, Pelican Bay's chief of police and certifiable closet redneck, had been the bane of my existence for the past fifteen years, so his attitude didn't surprise me. I scribbled the address Darcy gave me and hurried to dress.

Ten minutes later, with a bad case of bedhead and my body screaming for caffeine, I drove east along Main Street, deserted except for the crowded parking lot at the Blue Jay Sports Bar.

Pelican Bay, a picture-postcard retirement town and tourist mecca on Florida's central west coast, is populated primarily by retirees and snowbirds from the northern States and Canada, and few are night owls. Once the sun sets and television enters prime time, you might as well roll up the sidewalks, because no one ventures out—aside from a few of the younger folks and the occasional criminals.

The criminals are where I come in. I've been a cop for over twenty-two years and a detective with the Pelican Bay Police Department for the past fifteen, and being hauled out of bed after midnight was making early retirement seem more alluring by the minute.

The address Darcy had given me turned out to be a pizza place in a strip mall a few miles west of U.S. Highway 19, the main artery that bisected the county from Tarpon Springs at the north to the Sunshine Skyway Bridge at the mouth of Tampa Bay. All of the strip stores were dark except the center one, Mama Mia's Pizzeria. Lights blazed from the large plate-glass windows and illuminated a scattering of bistro tables and chairs in what was primarily a take-out joint.

I parked my twelve-year-old Volvo in a diagonal parking space between a Pelican Bay Police Department cruiser and the sheriff's crime scene unit van, clipped my shield to the pocket of my blazer and climbed out.

A crescent moon hung high in the east and palm fronds rustled above the parking median's lush floral landscaping, but a chill wind, compliments of a late November cold front, dispersed any semitropical illusions. I hurried into the pizzeria, as much to escape the cold as from any burning desire to fight crime.

Dave Adler, who'd been assigned as my partner at the beginning of the weight-loss clinic murders six weeks ago, met me at the door. Looking rested, bright-eyed and young enough to be my son, he greeted me with a grin. "How was your vacation, Detective Skerritt?"

At least I'd finally broken him of the habit of calling me "ma'am."

"Terrific," I lied.

During the past two weeks I'd spent several pleasant hours on the beaches of Caladesi Island and the deck of a cabin cruiser owned by Bill Malcolm, my former partner when I first became a cop with the Tampa P.D. twenty-two years ago. But for the remainder of my vacation, I'd been bored out of my gourd. Accustomed to working 24/7 in our understaffed CID—Criminal Investigation Department—for a decade and a half, I'd forgotten how to relax and enjoy myself. Without new or cold cases to occupy my mind, I had wandered my waterfront condo, restless and unable to concentrate, even on the popular novels I was so fond of.

"New hairdo?" Adler asked.

I resisted the urge to wipe the teasing grin off his too young, too handsome face. "What have we got?"

"Armed robbery."

"Anyone hurt?"

Adler shook his head. "The owner's shook up. She was the only one here."

"Mama Mia?"

He nodded, then jerked his head toward a door behind him. "She's back there."

I crossed the room, heavy with the smell of onions and Italian spices, rounded the take-out counter and entered the office at the back.

Steve Johnson, the patrolman who had responded to the 911 call, stood beside a woman who huddled in a desk chair and was trying to light a cigarette with trembling fingers. Johnson, big and beefy with a paunch that didn't need supplementing, stuffed the last of a slice of cold pizza into his mouth. "Hey, Maggie. Thith ith Maria Ridoletthi, th'owner."

"Maria Ridoletti?" I clarified. Johnson's full mouth had made me guess at the correct pronunciation.

Johnson swallowed hard. "Yeah. I'll be out front if you need me."

"Keep your hands in your pockets and your mouth closed. For all I know, you just consumed evidence." I smiled to take the bite out of my criticism. Johnson wasn't the brightest bulb in the chandelier, but his heart was in the right place. However, with the department under siege by a city council lobbying to shut us down and save taxpayer money by contracting with the county sheriff to take over policing Pelican Bay, we couldn't afford any screw-ups.

His pudgy face flushed with embarrassment, Johnson slid past me to the door and left me alone with Mama Mia.

"You want to tell me what happened?" I asked.

Maria Ridoletti was far from my image of an Italian mother. Midthirties, rake thin with stringy dark hair, narrow face and a body that looked as if she'd never eaten pizza or much of anything else, she stared up at me with dazed, black-lined eyes. "I was robbed."

"By a customer?"

She shook her head. "I'd already closed and locked up for the night. I was just beginning to count the day's receipts for the night deposit when I looked up and found him standing right where you are now. When he saw me, he jumped, like he hadn't expected anyone to be here."

"Was he someone you recognized?"

Maria nodded.

I dug deep for patience and asked, "Who was he?"

"Bill Clinton."

"Who?" Somewhere in my sleep-deprived brain, Bill Clinton's appearance at a pizza parlor made perfect sense. Especially since Mickey D's had closed for the night.

"You know," Maria said. "Bill Clinton, the former president."

I was about to call the CSU tech to bag what she was smoking when she explained.

"It was a mask, like on Halloween."

"A big man?"

She shook her head. "A runt, no bigger than me. But he kept one hand in his pocket and acted like he had a gun. So I didn't argue when he ordered me to hand over the cash."

"You're sure it was a man?"

She closed her eyes a moment, as if trying to remember, then nodded. "Yeah. No boobs, no butt. Scrawny neck with a big Adam's apple."

"Deep voice?"

"No, sort of squeaky."

"As if he was trying to disguise it?"

Maria shrugged. "Maybe."

"Did you see any identifying marks? Scars? Tattoos?"

"Except for his neck, he was pretty much covered up. Even wore gloves."

"What else was he wearing?"

"Jeans. A Buccaneer ball cap and sweatshirt. Black Nikes."

I couldn't help sighing. She'd just described the wardrobe of choice of almost half the men in the Tampa Bay area. "You said you locked the front door. Was the back locked, too?"

She nodded. "I always double check the doors before I count the money."

"So how did Mr. Clinton get in? You have any employees with keys?"

"No way. I can't pay much, so the turnover

here's pretty high. Don't have anyone I'd trust with keys." She took a long pull on her cigarette and exhaled.

I waved away the smoke. "Security system?"

She grimaced. "Never thought I needed one till now."

"How much did Clinton steal?"

"I hadn't finished counting. Most of our business is credit cards, but we sell a lot of pizza during Sunday football games. Had to be somewhere between six hundred and a thousand dollars." Her black-lined eyes misted with tears. "Times are tight, Detective. Will I get it back?"

Probably not. "We'll do our best."

"Detective Skerritt." Adler stood in the doorway. "Come look at this."

"You okay?" I asked Maria.

She swiped at her eyes with the back of one hand, smearing her eyeliner, then nodded and took another drag. I didn't have the heart to remind her about the state law that banned smoking in restaurants.

"Sit tight. I'll be right back." I left the room and followed Adler down a hallway that branched to the kitchen on the right, restrooms on the left. He shone his Maglite at the ceiling. Where the grate for the air-conditioning duct should have been was a gaping hole.

I groaned. "We've got ourselves a rooftop burglar."

I continued down the hall, pushed the panic bar on the rear exit and stepped outside. A gust of wind blew a tattered newspaper across the rear parking lot, empty except for a car I later learned was Ridoletti's. A dog barked in the distance. In the harsh glow of security lights, I scanned the back of the building. A Dumpster stood along the rear wall with a wooden pallet leaning against it. Another pallet atop the Dumpster rested against the wall like a ladder.

"There's your access," I said. "Make sure the techs process this area."

Fresh skid marks from a single narrow tire indicated the perp might have made his getaway by bike. Or it could have been a track left earlier in the day by a kid just passing through.

I nodded to the row of mobile homes in the trailer park that backed up to the strip mall. "We'll start a canvass. Maybe the neighbors saw something."

"Now?" Adler lifted his eyebrows in surprise. "It's almost 2:00 a.m."

"Most of those folks are in their late seventies and eighties," I reminded him. "They won't remember squat by daybreak."

"That's cold, Maggie."

"We're in a cold business, Adler."

Eight hours and an equal number of cups of coffee later, I sat at my desk in CID and typed my report. None of the neighbors behind Mama Mia's had seen or heard anything. Unlike the popular television crime dramas that have the culprit in custody within an hour—including commercial breaks—our crime lab techs had found zip, but not for lack of trying. To make matters worse, Maria Ridoletti was already proclaiming to all who would listen that if the sheriff's department had been handling the case, she'd probably have her money back by now.

I finished the report and tried to ignore the foreboding in my gut. Examining the strip mall, I'd noted that Bloomberg's Jewelers was next door to Mama Mia's. Maria had stated that the robber had been startled to encounter her. Apparently not expecting to confront anyone, however, he'd worn a mask, even though business hours were long over. That fact suggested he'd prepared for surveillance cameras, which were prevalent in Bloomberg's. My guess was that the thief had intended to hit the jewelry store but had become disoriented on the roof and picked the wrong air duct for entry.

If there was anything worse than a burglar, it was a stupid burglar. Maria Ridoletti was lucky he hadn't panicked and shot her. I figured the only reason he hadn't was that he hadn't actually had a gun.

This time.

"Skerritt! Get in here!" Chief Shelton's voice reverberated through the building from his office at the other end of the hall. Whenever his temper escalated, he abandoned the intercom for a more direct and intimidating form of communication.

Hoping to respond before his infamous temper boiled over, I hurried to his office. Kyle Dayton flashed me a sympathetic glance as I passed his post at the dispatch desk.

"Close the door," Shelton snapped when I entered his pine-paneled inner sanctum.

I shut the door behind me and waited for the chief to speak. For several weeks after the city council had first broached disbanding the police department, Shelton had discarded his fireball personality and slunk around the P.D. like a whipped dog. But somehow he'd regained his pugnacious attitude, the fiery spirit that had seen him through the Vietnam War and his early KKK days in the Georgia foothills and had ultimately made him a contender in the political arena. Politics was the only reason he held his $180,000 a year position, because Shelton had the policing and personnel skills of a gnat.

"You got a lead on this rooftop burglar?" Midmorning sunlight glinted off his bald head and his pale blue eyes squinted in the glare from the window that overlooked the city park.

"Not yet. No physical evidence was recovered at the scene, and the perp was masked."

"Dammit, Skerritt, first a serial murderer and now this. How the hell do you expect us to keep our department—"

"Crime happens, Chief. That's why we're here."

Shelton's face reddened and a vein bulged at his temple. "We're here to keep crime from happening, and if we don't, we sure as hell won't be here much longer. There'll be sheriff's cruisers patrolling these streets instead of our green-and-whites!"

"You want me to consult a psychic?" I already knew the answer, but Shelton's dumbfounded expression was worth asking the question.

"Hell, no. Just solve the damn case."

"With no suspects, no leads, no hard evidence, that's a problem. I could put the word out to our usual informants, offer to pay for info in case the perp blabs to his cronies or flashes his take around town."

Shelton shook his head with a guttural growl. "Whatever you do, keep expenses down. Money's the whole issue behind the council's push to can us."

"I'll do my best."

I turned to leave.

"And, Skerritt," he added.

"Yes?"

"Good luck."

"Thanks, Chief."

I knew he'd say that. Luck, after all, was free.

After fruitless hours of scanning mug shots and vital statistics in search of a runt who could fit through air ducts, I shut down my ancient computer and called it a day at 7:00 p.m.

Bill Malcolm met me at the Dock of the Bay, a restaurant and bar that overlooked the marina where Bill's thirty-eight-foot cabin cruiser, the *Ten-Ninety-Eight* was moored. Bill, who had lived on board since his retirement from the Tampa P.D. two years ago, had offered to cook supper for me in his galley kitchen, but I'd turned him down. Our relationship had taken an unexpected turn during my vacation. For years he had been joking about my marrying him, but now I wasn't so sure he was joking any longer, and I was uncertain how I felt about that change. I loved him, without question. One other fact of which I was completely certain, however, was that I wasn't a good candidate for marriage. In reality, no cop was, hence the skyrocketing divorce rate for police officers.

Years ago Bill's wife, spooked by fear of his dying in the line of duty, had divorced him and moved to Seattle with their only daughter, Melanie. Bill had been heartbroken. I'd stepped in to help with his daughter on her infrequent visits, and my relationship with Bill had deepened, then stalled in limbo when I'd put on the brakes. I still wasn't sure what had stopped me, fear of commitment or an equal anxiety over the true depth of Bill's feelings for me.

One thing was undeniable. Bill had been my best friend since our first days on patrol for the Tampa P.D. twenty-two years ago, and I didn't want anything to spoil that friendship. Tonight, although he'd been retired from the job for two years, I looked forward to hearing his take on my rooftop burglar.

I slid into a booth across from Bill. Toby Keith belted out "How Do You Like Me Now?" from the ancient Wurlitzer in the corner, and locals from the marina filled the stools at the bar and watched a pregame football show on the new plasma-screen television high on the wall in the corner.

Bill greeted me with a grin. His thick hair, once brown, was now white, a handsome contrast to his deep tan, and his blue eyes retained their boyish charm. "I already ordered."

"No problem." I always had an old-fashioned burger all the way with fries, and Bill was well versed in my preferences.

The waitress served frosted mugs of cold beer and when she left, Bill said, "For someone who just came off vacation, you look tired."

"I bet you say that to all the girls."

"You also look beautiful," he hastened to add, "but I'm worried about you. You wore yourself out on the weight-loss clinic murders. I was hoping with those solved, you might slow down a bit."

"No rest for the weary." I sipped my beer and hoped it wouldn't send me into a deep coma.

While we waited for our food, I gave Bill the details on our rooftop burglar. "Looks like I've hit a wall," I said when I'd finished.

"Have you tried tracking the Clinton mask?"

"Adler worked on it all day. But the masks were produced over a decade ago and carried by the thousands by Wal-Mart and K-Mart, as well as other specialty stores. Nobody kept records on individual purchases of the masks. Besides, you know how many transients and new residents we have in this county. That mask could have been brought in from anywhere in the country."

"What about online?"

"I'll make sure Adler checked that, too." I hated computers, didn't own one and barely tolerated using the one at work. In a profession becoming increasingly high tech, my technophobia was another compelling reason to toss in the towel. I refused to own a cell phone and only reluctantly carried a beeper.

Our meals arrived and as I bit into my burger with gusto, I realized I'd forgotten to eat lunch. Good thing, since the food in front of me represented an entire day's ration. Fresh memories of three overweight murder victims had me counting calories.

Bill put down his burger and wiped his lips with his napkin. "Margaret—"

Besides Bill, only members of my immediate family called me Margaret. When I'd first partnered with him, he'd called me Princess Margaret, a derogatory reference to my debutante days, but after I saved his life during a domestic dispute call, I'd won his respect and he'd referred to me as Skerritt on the job. Later, after his divorce, when our relationship developed outside of work, he'd begun calling me Margaret, often with a tenderness I found hard to resist.

"Margaret, I've given this a lot of thought." His blue eyes locked gazes with mine and his expression was deadly serious.

My heartbeat stuttered. Had my unwavering rejections of his marriage proposals convinced him to move on?

"I've decided," he continued, "to accept your invitation to have Thanksgiving at your mother's."

"That wasn't an invitation," I said, relieved only until the prospect of Bill and my mother in the same room hit me. "That was a threat."

"She can't be that bad."

"She doesn't approve of anything about me," I

countered. "And she lets me know it every time our paths cross."

My mother was a social scion of Pelican Bay. Her father had been a prominent physician, my late father a distinguished cardiologist, and she enjoyed her position of wealth and influence. When I had graduated from college with a degree in library science and announced my engagement to Greg Singleford, who was completing his internship in the ER, Mother had been over the moon. But Greg's brutal murder by a crack addict in an ER treatment room had changed everything.

I'd loved Greg with all the passion and innocence of youth, and his death had shaken my core values. As a result, I couldn't see spending my life with books, or, as my mother had intended, at meetings of the Junior League and Art Guild, once I'd realized that the world was such a dangerous place. Daddy had supported my decision to enter the police academy and had openly expressed his pride in my accomplishments. He'd served as a buffer between Mother and me until his death twelve years ago. But Mother had been horrified from the beginning that her younger daughter had chosen a down-and-dirty career in law enforcement over social prestige. And she never let me forget it. During the recent publicity over my arrest of Lester Morelli for the clinic murders, she'd taken to her bed with a sick headache and had remained there until after Morelli had been indicted and the news coverage had ceased.

"So you're withdrawing the invitation?" Bill asked.

"No, I'm just warning you that dinner with Mother will be an ordeal. It always is. So you might want to reconsider."

He reached across the table and grasped my hand. "Maybe just once you ought to tell your mother to take her hoity-toity attitude and stick it up her—"

"Bill!"

"You've heard the word *ass* before," he said with a rare flash of temper. "You've even used it a few times yourself."

"But never in relation to my mother. Mother wouldn't be caught dead with a common ass. She has only a very sophisticated derriere." I teased to defuse his irritation.

"You've got to stop tiptoeing around her."

"She and Caroline are all the family I have."

Pain flashed through his eyes, and I wished I

could take back my words. Bill had even less family than I did.

He took a deep breath and exhaled. "Maybe it's time for a family of your own. We could be a family, you and I."

I was on the verge of choking up over his proposal when my beeper sounded. "I have to call the station."

"I'm giving you a cell phone for Christmas," he promised with a scowl.

"I'd either lose it or forget to charge it, so save your money." I hurried from the table to the pay phone in the lobby.

I was gone only a couple of minutes before I returned and cast a longing look at my unfinished burger. "Gotta go," I said. "Another break-in."

"You're dead on your feet," Bill said. "At least let me drive."

For a few seconds I luxuriated in the unaccustomed comfort of having someone fuss over me. Then duty kicked in.

"Okay, but let's roll. Shelton was already frothing at the mouth over last night's burglary. I don't want him putting me on report for slow response."

CHAPTER 2

Last night's burglar may have been stupid, but if he was hoping to make the Pelican Bay Police Department look bad, tonight's repeat break-in had definitely accomplished that goal. Bill parked his car in the same space I'd used the night before. I thanked him for the ride and left the car in a hurry. I didn't know whether to feel relieved or disappointed that our discussion about families had been interrupted. Relieved, I decided. Being with Bill when he was relaxed and laid-back was easy. When the serious stuff kicked in, I was out of my element.

It was just after 8:00 p.m., and light poured from the windows of Mama Mia's, doing a booming take-out business, judging by the activity visible through the plate glass and the number of drivers scurrying from the restaurant with insulated bags. Monday night football apparently created a huge appetite for pizza.

My attention this evening, however, wasn't on Mama Mia's but Bloomberg's Jewelers next door. Steve Johnson let me in the front entrance.

"The owner's on his way," Johnson said. "It was a smash-and-grab."

Shards of glass from several display cases littered the narrow aisle. Bloomberg's wasn't a large store, but its small space packed a hefty inventory of high-end goods. Even my very picky mother was a frequent shopper here. Looking at the empty display cases, I hoped Bloomberg's insurance was adequate. The man had lost a mint.

"We have to quit meeting like this, Maggie." Adler appeared at my elbow and handed me a large foam cup of coffee. "Malcolm sent you this. Got it at Mama Mia's."

I took the steaming infusion of caffeine with gratitude and glanced toward the parking lot where Bill had returned to his car and was now reading a magazine in the glow of the dome light. It was going to be another long night.

Bloomberg arrived immediately after Adler. He entered the shop and, for a moment, I feared the little man would burst into tears.

"I'm Detective Skerritt," I said. "We spoke on the phone this morning."

A frail, nondescript man with kind brown eyes and graying hair, Bloomberg wrung his hands. "You warned me, Detective. And I called the contractor. He's scheduled tomorrow morning to secure the ducts on the roof. Too late now."

Bloomberg seemed to shrink into his shapeless gray sweater as he shook his head and surveyed the damage. Adler moved toward the rear of the shop and entered a hallway.

"Can you tell me what's missing?" I asked Bloomberg.

"Someone knew what he was doing," the jeweler said. "He took only the most expensive items."

"Didn't have much time, though," Johnson chimed in. "I was in the neighborhood and was here within minutes of the alarm sounding."

Adler returned to the front room. "Entered through the roof, just like last night."

"Do you have motion detectors?" I asked Bloomberg.

The elderly man shook his head. "Only alarms on the doors and display windows."

"Were the interior lights on when you arrived?" I asked Johnson.

He shook his head. "I hit the lights when I got here so I could see to turn off the alarm."

"Then our burglar couldn't be seen from the street," I said, "and he didn't set off the alarm until he left. He had all the time in the world to pick and choose what he wanted."

The CSU techs arrived. "Déjà vu all over again," one commented before starting to work.

"I'll need your surveillance tapes," I told Bloomberg.

"From how far back?" he asked.

"How far back do you keep them?"

He looked chagrined. "My wife makes fun of me. Says I'm obsessive/compulsive. It takes a lot of tapes, but I keep them for a month. Just in case."

"In case?"

His lined cheeks reddened with embarrassment. "I'm an old man. Sometimes I don't notice things like I should. If something was missing, like from a shoplifter, it could be days before I'd notice." His eyes brightened. "But if I have the tapes, I can at least go back and see what happened."

"Let me have them all."

I'd begin with the past few hours. I was hopeful surveillance would reveal a good view of our burglar. Even if masked, if he was a habitual offender, I might recognize him. If not, I'd work my way

backward through the remaining videos. If someone had cased the store in the past month, he
probably wouldn't have bothered to hide his face
and I'd have him on tape.

Several hours later I wasn't feeling as confident.
I'd returned to the station to view the most recent
surveillance video. Even in the dim light from the
streetlights outside, it had captured perfect images
of the burglar, who had ditched Bill Clinton for a
ski mask. After the pizzeria closed, Maria Ridoletti
stopped by the station to confirm our perp. Standing in front of the monitor, she watched the tape
and shook her head.

"That's not him."

"You mean, it's not Clinton?" I suspected that
the ski mask had thrown her.

She crossed her arms over her skinny chest and
tapped her foot impatiently. "It's a different guy al-
together. He's almost a foot taller than the one
who robbed me."

Those were words I didn't want to hear. "You're
sure? After all, you were sitting down."

"And the guy in the Clinton mask was almost
eye-to-eye with me. Nope, that's definitely not the

one who robbed me." Her scathing look spoke volumes. "Looks like you've got two robbers to catch now."

The next morning the insistent ringing of the telephone awakened me. A glance at my bedside clock indicated the time was a few minutes past seven. I'd had less than four hours' sleep in the past two days, and I wanted nothing more than to let the answering machine pick up while I dived under the covers until the alarm sounded at seven-thirty. But, recalling the dynamic duo of thieves still at large, I fumbled for the phone beside my bed and braced to hear Darcy announcing another break-in.

"Good morning, dear." My mother's refined voice, buoyant with irritating cheerfulness, resonated in my ear. "I was hoping I'd find you at home."

That one simple statement carried a truckload of disapproval, her indirect snipe at the unpredictable hours of my job.

"What's up?" I asked. Mother never called simply to chat or pass the time of day. She communicated only to issue a summons or an edict. This morning was no exception.

"I'm calling about Thanksgiving dinner. You are coming, aren't you?"

"I certainly intend to." I didn't want to get into the possibility, of which Mother was well aware but chose to ignore, that work might intervene.

"We'll gather at five for cocktails. Dinner at six."

With partial consciousness came the memory of my conversation with Bill at the restaurant the previous night. "If it's all right, I'd like to bring a guest."

"A guest?" Her voice crackled with surprise.

"Bill Malcolm."

"Oh."

"Is that a problem?"

"Of course not." Her tone contradicted her words. "But, really, Margaret, what do you know about this man?"

"*This man* was my partner for seven years and he's been my friend for over twenty." The fact that in all that time he'd never met my family said a lot about my shaky relationship with them.

"I'm aware of that, dear," she said with a hint of exasperation, "but what do you *know* about him?"

"I know that he's good and decent, but if you'd rather I came alone—"

"I'm sure Mr. Malcolm is a very nice man, but what do you know about his *family?*" For Mother, with people, as with art and antiques, provenance was all.

"Most of them are dead," I said.

"Don't be obtuse, Margaret. You know exactly what I'm asking. Who *were* they?"

Decent, unpretentious, hardworking people, with whom my elitist mother had absolutely nothing in common. "His father was a citrus grower in Plant City. He's eighty-five, suffers from Alzheimer's, and is in an assisted-living facility in Tampa."

"He was a farmer?"

"You could say that." Contrariness kept me silent on the fact that Bill's father's orange groves were several thousand acres of prime real estate, worth millions if sold for development. A sufficient amount of wealth covered a multitude of sins in Mother's book, but I wasn't about to pander to her prejudices.

"And his son lives in Pelican Bay?" She was sounding more dubious by the minute.

"At the marina. On his boat."

"Mr. Malcolm lives on a boat?" Horror laced her voice. "Like a transient?"

Even in my sleep-deprived state, I experienced a guilty thrill at Mother's disapproval. I'd learned long ago I could never please her, so sometimes I took perverse pleasure in pushing her buttons instead. Especially since I was still smarting from her dismissive attitude a few weeks ago at the yacht club when I'd saved her from an armed teenager intent on robbery. Instead of thanking me, she'd criticized my language. Why I, at forty-eight, still longed for my mother's approval, was one of the mysteries of the universe.

"Because he does live on a boat, I'm sure he'd enjoy having Thanksgiving dinner in a real home," I lied, knowing Bill could whip up an elegant holiday meal in his small galley kitchen that would put Mother's expensive caterers to shame.

"Your friends are always welcome at my house, Margaret," Mother insisted, but her tone lacked conviction. "I'll be happy to have Mr. Malcolm join us for Thanksgiving. But please, remind him that we dress for dinner."

I stifled the irrational image of Mother, my perfect older sister Caroline and her stuffy husband, Hunt, sitting naked around Mother's antique dining table, and I couldn't resist baiting her. "Clothes

are always helpful, especially when the weather's
chilly."

Mother's sigh of exasperation vibrated loudly
through the handset. "You know what I mean,
Margaret. At least, I hope you haven't forgotten
all the social niceties."

Not as long as I had Mother as a constant reminder. "Thanks, Mother. I'll see you Thursday."

I climbed out of bed and gazed through the sliding-glass doors of my second-floor bedroom at St.
Joseph Sound and the Intracoastal Waterway that
separated the city from Pelican Beach. The waters,
smooth as glass, reflected a towering bank of cu-
mulus clouds, rose-tipped by the sunrise, and mirrored the shimmering lavender-and-pink striations
cast by the early-morning sky.

For a moment I considered what life might be
like without my job. With the tidy sum vested in
my pension and a small income from the trust
Daddy had left me, I wouldn't have to work. If I
retired, I could enjoy a cup of coffee and the morning paper on my balcony while I watched the char-
ter boats heading into the Gulf with their
boatloads of tourists.

And then what would I do the rest of the day?

With a month's worth of Bloomberg's surveillance video waiting at the station, I headed for the shower.

Adler was already at the station when I arrived. "Did you go home last night?" I asked.

Adler had a pretty young wife, Sharon, and an adorable year-old daughter, Jessica, and I worried that the extra hours he logged were negatively affecting his family. I didn't want him to end up as Bill had, divorced and unable to watch his daughter growing up.

"Yeah, I left right after you." Adler flushed to the tips of his ears. "I'm logging some personal time today. Came in early to let you know before I take off."

He was having trouble looking me in the eye. I shut the door to the CID cubicle that some called an office and faced him. "What's up?"

He lowered his voice. "An interview with the Clearwater P.D. I can't wait for the council to make up its mind about whether to keep our department. For my family's sake, I have to make sure I have a job."

Although he was still green, I respected Adler more than any of my partners since Bill Malcolm. With his sharp mind and humble demeanor, he had the makings of a great detective. He also had the rare gift of bringing out my maternal instincts, and I would sorely miss him if he left.

I spent the rest of the day watching surveillance tapes until my eyes crossed. During the past few weeks, several people had done some serious browsing in Bloomberg's without making any purchases, but no one fit the description of either of the perps. In desperation, I punched the number of Mick Rafferty, head of the sheriff's crime lab, into my phone.

"Mick," I said when he answered. "Do you have the latest face recognition software?"

"You know I do, Maggie, me darlin'." Mick was quintessential Boston Irish, young and cocky with devilish blue eyes, wall-to-wall freckles and an encyclopedic mind like a steel trap. "Haven't you seen the ACLU goon squad screaming invasion of privacy for the past few months on the evening news?"

I wasn't about to admit how long it had been since I'd watched a newscast, evening or otherwise. "Does the software work?"

"What have you got?"

I explained about the surveillance tapes and my hope that Mick could run a few of the faces through the system in hopes of coming up with a match.

"Make notes of the footage you want me to check and send me the videos," he said. "But I have to warn you, I have three major homicide cases that have priority. It could be a while before I can get to your tapes."

"I understand, Mick," I said. "But I'm flying blind here, and I'm afraid this pair will hit again. Next time somebody might get hurt."

"You'll get the bastards, Maggie. You always do."

I marked the tapes that showed suspicious customers, bundled the videos in a bag and carried them to my car to transport to the sheriff's crime lab in midcounty.

Thanksgiving morning dawned warm, clear and bright, the kind of November day that had the folks down at the chamber of commerce—and tourists who'd shelled out big bucks for their holiday vacations—exchanging high fives. As I drove north along Edgewater Drive into town, joggers in colorful spandex were spaced along the bayside path like beads on a string, the brown pelicans that gave the town its name dived for fish in the emerald-green waters, and the cloudless sky promised a balmy, sunny day.

After I passed the marina, I turned into the parking lot of Sophia's, a four-star restaurant and hotel, built like a Venetian palazzo and nestled on the edge of the bay. Antonio Stavropoulos, the maître d', had called the station earlier and requested that I stop by, and the dispatcher had relayed his message.

I had to circle the lot twice before I found a place to park. Thanksgiving breakfast at Sophia's was a local holiday tradition, and the recent murder of the restaurant's owner by her greedy husband had apparently not diminished the eatery's appeal. If anything, the publicity appeared to have increased business.

Antonio met me in the lobby. The tall, elegant man, gray-haired and rake slim in his continental-cut suit, took a large cardboard box from behind the hostess desk and handed it to me.

"A gift," he said, "for the members of your department from the staff at Sophia's."

Departmental regs and Shelton with apoplexy danced through my head. "I'm sorry, but we can't accept gifts."

"But today is Thanksgiving, and here we are

grateful for the hard work the police have done to catch our Sophia's killer and put Lester Morelli behind bars where he belongs."

"You're very kind," I said, "but rules are rules."

And Chief Shelton was poised like a stalking panther, waiting for one wrong slip so he could fire me and justify his fierce opposition to my joining the force fifteen years ago, when I'd taken him to court in a discrimination suit to win my job.

"I understand," Antonio said with a twinkle in his eye. "Then you must purchase these pastries for your department, no?"

I stifled a groan. Pastries at Sophia's ran about a dollar a bite, and that huge box held at least four dozen of the luscious goodies. "Sure. How much?"

"One dollar," Antonio said with a deadpan expression. "Tax included."

Ten minutes later, with the box of baklava and other Greek delicacies stashed in the station's break room, I entered my office to contemplate the rooftop burglars who'd so far eluded me.

The fact that they hadn't struck again the past two nights was no consolation. I'd asked the chief to have the media alert business owners to secure their rooftop duct systems, but Shelton was too paranoid about the political fallout to comply. The most I'd been able to accomplish was the distribution of lists of the stolen jewelry along with our incomplete description of the thieves to Bay area pawnshops. My only hope was that the perps would be dumb enough to try to move the items in the area.

Later in the morning, Adler was plowing his way through a third piece of baklava and revisiting mug shots in case we'd missed someone the first time around. He'd offered no details on his earlier job interview, and I hadn't asked. I figured he'd talk about it when he was ready.

"How come there are so few skinny criminals?" he asked as he flipped through the pages of photographs. "All these guys are big and muscle-bound."

I shrugged. "They've all been through the system. Guess they bulked up by working out in prison. Unless…"

"Unless what?"

My mind didn't want to grasp the possibility that had been flitting around the edges of my consciousness since Maria Ridoletti's description of the first perp.

"Unless our thieves are children."

CHAPTER 3

I dressed for the holiday dinner at Mother's with my usual fatalism. No matter how well-made or perfectly fitted my gray slacks, burgundy silk blouse and ubiquitous black blazer, Mother and Caroline, who were on a first-name basis with every salesclerk in Neiman Marcus at Tampa's International Plaza, would consider me a frump.

But focusing on couture was merely a diversion from the anger over the break-ins that simmered deep inside, a fire I had to douse or I'd end up being the turkey at our Thanksgiving meal. Interacting with my family without creating a domestic crisis took the combined skills of a global diplomat and a SWAT hostage negotiator. In my present state of mind, I'd send my mother into cardiac arrest and my sister into a swoon before the night ended.

Bill Malcolm, who, like Sean Connery, grew

more handsome with age, arrived at four-thirty, looking like a cover model for *Yachting World* in gray slacks, navy blazer and a white turtleneck that showcased his George Hamilton tan. Homing in on my disposition like a heat-seeking missile, he saw immediately beneath my calm facade.

"If this dinner has you so worked up, don't go," he stated with his usual and often irritating logic.

"It's not that."

"The job?"

I nodded. "You'd think after two decades I'd grow a thicker skin."

"Uh-uh." He took my hand, led me to the sofa and pulled me down beside him. "If these crimes stop affecting you, then you've lost your humanity. I never want to see that happen."

"I can deal with most of it, but when kids are involved…"

Images that had dogged my days and haunted my dreams for over sixteen years made me shudder. Small, white, bloated bodies on the medical examiner's table, young girls, children really, pulled from Tampa Bay, where they'd been dumped like garbage by their assailants. Try as we might, Bill and I had been unable to track down the monster who had killed them. The murders had stopped, but whether because we'd turned up the heat or the killer had simply moved on, I'd probably never know.

"New case?" Bill asked.

"Not exactly. It just struck me today that our rooftop burglars might be kids."

Bill nodded. "And a kid didn't have the knowledge to pull off that jewelry store heist, not unless someone coached him."

"What kind of person uses kids to do his dirty work?" Dickens' *Oliver Twist* and Fagin came instantly to mind. I knew that degree in library science was good for something.

"You sure they're kids?" Bill asked.

"I don't have hard evidence, only what my gut's telling me."

He pulled me toward him and kissed my forehead. "Ah, Margaret, that's only one of the things I love about you."

"My gut?"

"That, too, but mainly because after over twenty years on the job, you're still capable of outrage."

I glanced at the clock. "Speaking of outrage, if we don't get moving, that's what Mother's going to display if we're late."

* * *

The home of my youth was located in Pelican Bay's most exclusive section, Belle Terre, a waterfront enclave of mansions built in the 1920s and 1930s on a bluff above the sound, most now on the National Register of Historic Buildings.

Growing up, I'd taken for granted the Mediterranean splendor of the house designed by Misner with its soaring beamed ceilings, mosaic tile floors, central courtyard and Spanish tile roof, set on two acres of prime waterfront real estate. In the lush St. Augustine lawn, brick pathways meandered through moss-draped live oaks, orange trees and jacarandas, and ended at the bayside tennis court, where I'd spent some of the happiest hours of my childhood playing tennis with my dad. Today I couldn't remember the last time I'd held a racket.

Bill gave a low whistle of surprise as he guided his car along the winding drive to the front of the house. "These are pretty fancy digs."

"When I was living here, I never thought of this place as extraordinary. My friends lived in similar houses, so this was no big deal."

He brought the car to a halt next to my brother-in-law Hunt's Lincoln Town Car. "You miss your debutante days?"

I thought for a moment, as much to postpone going inside as to consider his question. "I miss the innocence. In spite of so many advantages, I led a very sheltered life. My friends didn't do drugs or have drunken parties. And there was no premarital sex." I flashed him a smile. "We were snobs, but we were virtuous snobs."

"You're still virtuous." His answering smile was warm and intimate.

"You know better." My wild and hot affair with a fellow cop my first year on the Tampa P.D. had been no secret. I'd hoped the physical intimacy would dull my emotional pain, but I'd soon discovered that hard work was a better analgesic than sex and had quickly ended the involvement.

"Our parents didn't divorce," I continued. "If there was scandal, it was kept so hush-hush, we never knew about it. And even though the Vietnam War was raging and the country was mired in antiwar and civil-rights protests and riots, none of it touched me. I thought I lived in a perfect world, until…"

Bill squeezed my hand. He'd heard many times the story of Greg's murder and how the trauma and anger over that horrific event had propelled me into a career in law enforcement.

"After all this—" Bill's gesture took in the impressive two-story house and sprawling grounds that required a team of gardeners to maintain them "—the academy must have been a culture shock."

I nodded. "And, in the words of Thomas Wolfe, I can't go home again. I'll never look at the world the same."

"You went from one extreme to the other. Maybe it's time to find a middle ground."

He was talking about retirement, and the prospect held a certain seductiveness, until I remembered the possibility that some scumbag might be using kids to do his dirty work. "Not yet."

"More dragons to slay?" He squeezed my hand again and his blue eyes lit with amusement.

"How were you able to finally give it up?" I asked.

His expression sobered. "One day I woke up and knew I'd had enough, that I didn't want to live surrounded by crime and the misery it inflicts any longer. So I just walked away."

"You think that'll happen to me?"

"There's always hope."

I noted then the other cars beyond Hunt's and realized we'd been the last to arrive. "Speaking of dragons, we should hurry inside before the Queen Mother starts breathing fire."

Estelle, mother's longtime maid, dressed in her usual black uniform and an immaculate starched apron as white as her hair, opened the massive carved front door. "Happy Thanksgiving, Miss Margaret. It's good to see you home again."

I hugged her and kissed her smooth ebony cheek. Her scent of Ivory soap triggered a hundred memories. Mother would have had a cow if she'd witnessed my display of affection toward the hired help, but Estelle had raised me, bandaged my scraped knees, dried my childhood tears, fed me cookies after school and, years later, held me when my father died. In many ways, she'd been more of a mother than my biological one.

"Happy Thanksgiving, Estelle. I've missed you. This is my friend Bill Malcolm."

Bill shook Estelle's hand and her bright brown eyes scanned him up and down with the scrutiny of a cattle buyer in a stockyard. "He's a keeper, Miss Margaret."

"Thanks, Estelle," Bill said. "That's what I've been trying to tell her."

"Your mamma and the rest of 'em are in the

courtyard," Estelle said. "I gots to check on them caterers before they trash my kitchen."

She hurried toward the back of the house at a shuffling gait that indicated her bunions were bothering her, and I guided Bill through the foyer into the courtyard.

"Wow," Bill murmured as we stepped into the soaring atrium. "Great space."

Seeing the courtyard through his eyes made me reevaluate where I'd played as a child. A triple-tiered fountain anchored the center of the huge expanse of Mexican terra-cotta tiles. Tropical plantings of frangipani, gardenias, bird of paradise, and travelers' palms softened the corners of the huge area. Open hallways with Moorish arches circled both the first and second floors, and an arching glass ceiling flooded the area with natural light and kept the air-conditioning in and the weather out.

Groupings of wrought-iron chairs and tables with plump cushions were scattered in conversational clusters across the open area. With unusual grace for an eighty-two-year-old, Mother rose from a nearby chair and came to greet us.

"I thought perhaps you weren't coming," she

said in a benevolent tone that didn't entirely hide her disapproval of our tardiness.

The coolness of her greeting was in stark contrast to the bear hug and resounding kisses my father would have offered and made me realize one of the reasons I hated coming home was the fact that Daddy was no longer there to welcome me.

A muscle ticked in Bill's cheek, the only indication that Mother's attitude had annoyed him. He seldom showed anger, not because he didn't feel it, but because he'd learned over the years to effectively leash his deep rage, an appropriate response to the injustices he'd encountered on the job and in his personal life. I watched as he somehow managed to bleed the tension from his body and relax, a skill I envied.

"If we're late, Mrs. Skerritt," Bill said, "it's my fault. I lingered too long admiring the beautiful grounds of your house. A fitting prelude, I might add, to its exquisite interior."

Mother's stiff demeanor softened slightly. "You must be Mr. Malcolm."

"Please, call me Bill." He gave her his warmest smile, the one that had caused hardened criminals to spill their guts in the interview rooms, and grasped her hand in both of his. I watched in amazement as the Iron Magnolia succumbed to his charm, a quality that made Bill irresistible. He had, hands down, the best people skills of anyone I'd ever met.

"And you must call me Priscilla," she insisted.

I almost swallowed my tongue. Mother rarely allowed anyone to call her by her first name. In fact, I'd heard it so seldom, I'd almost forgotten it.

"Priscilla," Bill said. "It suits you. Very regal."

Mother did appear regal in her floor-length skirt of black taffeta, a high-necked, white silk blouse with long sleeves, a cummerbund in gold-and-black plaid, and her snowy hair piled high like a crown.

Leaving me trailing in their wake, she escorted Bill deeper into the courtyard to meet the usual suspects. My sister, Caroline, looking like a younger clone of Mother in both dress and hairstyle, although her tresses were a golden bottle-blond, sipped a martini and eyed Bill with interest over the rim of her glass. Her husband, Huntington Yarborough, a big man whose usual florid complexion had turned an even deeper red after a few drinks, rose from his seat by the fountain where he was nursing what looked to be a double Scotch.

Michelle, their oldest daughter, and her husband, Chad, hovered in a far corner with my nephew Robert and his wife, Sandra. My four great-nieces and great-nephews were conspicuously absent, either at home with a sitter or farmed out to their other grandparents. Mother was adamant that small children had no place at social functions, not even family holiday celebrations.

Bill, well-versed in my family tree and its twisted branches, met and greeted each of my relatives with his usual ease. A waiter appeared and took our drink orders.

"So," Bill said to Hunt, "Margaret tells me you're in the insurance business."

I suppressed a groan. Once Hunt began talking business, there was no stopping him. I'd dozed through many of his dinner-table monologues.

Hunt pounced on Bill like a puppy on a bone. "You name it, I insure it. Property and casualty, life and health, annuities. I can do all your financial planning—"

Someone grasped my elbow and a familiar voice said, "How are you, Margaret? I haven't seen you in too many years."

Seton Fellows, Daddy's best friend, smiled down at me from his extraordinary height of six foot five. The best neurologist in the Tampa Bay area, the man was a giant in the medical profession, as my father had been. His thinning gray hair matched his deep gray eyes, but the age that lined his face hadn't affected his erect posture or his usually sunny disposition.

"What a nice surprise, Dr. Fellows. Mother didn't tell me you were coming."

"It was a last-minute invitation," he said with a conspiratorial wink. "Your mother needed an even number at the table."

Bill's last-minute inclusion had thrown off Mother's seating arrangement. "Lucky for us," I assured him. "How have you been?"

His gray eyes clouded. "Lonely. This will be my first Thanksgiving without Nancy. So it's good to be with friends."

"You've known Mother and Daddy a long time, haven't you?"

He nodded and sipped his drink. "Philip and I were in medical school together."

Across the courtyard, Mother and Caroline hung on Hunt's every word, and somehow even Bill managed to appear interested. With Dr. Fellows as my captive audience, I had found someone who might satisfy my curiosity about my parents' early years, a time neither had discussed, at least, not with me. Their large wedding portrait hung in the sitting room of the master suite, but neither Mother nor Daddy had ever talked about the few years prior to or immediately following their marriage.

"What were they like then?" I asked Seton.

"Your parents?"

I nodded. "Before Daddy became Pelican Bay's best cardiologist."

The lines in his face crinkled with amusement. "Philip, as all of us, worked long, hard hours."

"And Mother?"

His hesitation was brief but notable. "She organized the wives' association. Not many female medical students in those days. Why do you ask?"

I shrugged. "They were so different from each other. I never could understand the attraction."

"They complemented each other, like yin and yang. Your mother took charge of everything outside of work, which freed your father to be the brilliant doctor that he was."

"Did they love each other?"

"They were married for almost fifty years."

"Were they happy?"

"Happiness means different things to different people."

He had sidestepped my question, but before I could rephrase it, Mother rang a small silver bell with all the drama of a stage production, and Dr. Fellows hurried to escort her into the adjacent dining room.

The florist and caterers had transformed the room. I pictured a television reality show, "How the Rich and Famous Celebrate Thanksgiving," as I observed the towering topiaries of chrysanthemums, colorful autumn leaves and deep green ivy that marched down the center of the massive refectory table that had once graced an ancient Spanish monastery. Gigantic cornucopia, overflowing with fruits and gourds, flanked the silver serving dishes on the matching sideboard. The table was set with Mother's heavy silver flatware and engraved napkin rings and covered with enough white damask for a circus tent.

We stood behind our chairs, waiting for Mother to be seated. I thought longingly of the weathered pine table in the sunny kitchen and wished Bill and I could share our meal there with Estelle.

Mother rang her silver bell again. "Dr. Fellows will say grace."

Before I bowed my head, I caught a sympathetic

look from Bill, who had been assigned the seat across from me.

"Heavenly Father," Dr. Fellows began.

The beeper on my belt shrilled, shattering the room's quiet.

"Really, Margaret," Mother said with no effort to hide her disapproval. "Can't you turn that thing off?"

Dr. Fellows smiled, but Caroline, Michelle and Sandra glared with as much disapproval as if I'd just stripped topless.

"I'm on call, Mother. If you'll excuse me, I'll use the phone in the foyer. Please, go ahead. Don't wait for me."

I'd have felt relief at being snatched from the jaws of social responsibility, but I knew a summons on a holiday had to be bad news.

I was right.

Darcy Wilkins answered at dispatch when I phoned the station. "We've got a drowning at a private residence on the beach."

"Accidental?"

"It's your call," she said. "The M.E.'s on her way."

She gave me the address. I braced for Mother's disapproval and returned to the dining room to announce my regrets.

CHAPTER 4

Bill dropped me off at my condo, where I picked up my car for the trek to the beach. As I drove across the causeway, I saw that the city crews had already strung Christmas lights and decorations, and their festive glitter provided an ironic contrast to my mission. Even if the reported drowning turned out to be accidental, one family would have their future Thanksgiving holidays marred forever by memories of tragedy.

The causeway emptied into the commercial district of the beach, high-rise hotels and condos, restaurants, fishing piers and dozens of shops crammed with T-shirts and tacky tourist souvenirs made in Taiwan. The streets were crowded with out-of-state and rental cars and the sidewalks filled with folks who had forfeited the traditions of home for a holiday in the sun.

I turned north and the asphalt of the commercial district gave way to ancient brick streets. Homes, modest in size and style but worth a small fortune because of their beach location, lined the roadway. The street ended at a huge wrought-iron gate, more symbolic than obstructive, since it always stood open. It marked the entrance to the beach's most upscale residential area, Yacht Club Estates. I drove past the clubhouse where, a few weeks ago, I'd apprehended two armed punks attempting to rob my mother. Most of the houses were screened from the road by massive hedges, since their coveted views came from the Intracoastal Waterway on the east side of the street or the white sand beaches of the Gulf of Mexico on the west. The price of real estate on this end of the beach started at seven figures, then soared like a bottle rocket.

A few blocks past the yacht club, another ornate gate loomed, this barrier the real deal with an electronic surveillance system and pass-card entry. Tonight, however, the usually locked gates stood ajar. Death, the great leveler, hadn't needed a key to infiltrate this bastion of the wealthy.

I drove through the open portal and approached the cluster of vehicles gathered on the beach side of the street. A P.B.P.D. green-and-white and a paramedics' van stood with their emergency lights strobing the adjacent sea grape hedges with flashes of red and blue. Adler's SUV was parked beside the cruiser. After I climbed from my car, he met me at the break in the hedge.

"I'd hoped we'd get through the day without a call," he said. "No such luck."

"Did you miss dinner?" I asked.

He shook his head. "We ate early, so I'm missing only football games and the washing up. How about you?"

"No big deal." I felt only a momentary twinge of guilt over the fact that I'd rather work a signal seven than have Thanksgiving with my relatives. "Who's the vic?"

"Vincent Lovelace."

"The cable channel giant?"

"Founder and owner of Your Vacation Channel. And from the looks of this house, this guy didn't need a vacation. He lived one."

"He's on permanent holiday now."

Adler nodded. "Paramedics pronounced him when they arrived. Doc Cline's on the way."

We stepped through the gate in the hedge and the house, a huge four-story tower of glass and steel with lights blazing from every level, rose in front of me. I could see through the rooms of the first floor to the brightly illuminated terrace with its lap pool and the beach and Gulf beyond. On the pool deck lay the body of Vincent Lovelace. Rudy Beaton, a P.B.P.D. patrol officer, was taking statements from two paramedics. A woman with wet hair sat huddled in a blanket on a deck chair on a raised terrace at the north end of the pool.

I recognized Mrs. Lovelace instantly. Until that moment, I'd forgotten that Vincent had married Samantha Weston, daughter of Mother's best friend Isabelle. With a sinking feeling, I knew, no matter how this investigation sorted out, Mother was not going to be happy.

I walked through the house with its minimalist furnishings, enough vibrant splashes of primary colors for a Jackson Pollock canvas or a day-care center, and immaculate housekeeping. The whole place looked as if it had been staged for a photography shoot for a spread in *Architectural Digest*. Classical music, a Vivaldi mandolin concerto, flowed from surround-sound speakers and blended with the crash of the surf from the adjacent beach. Sandalwood-scented candles glowed on the fireplace mantel and coffee table but couldn't quite mask the cooking aromas from an earlier meal.

Adler and I stepped onto the patio where Rudy met us.

"The wife called 911," he said. "Said she found her husband on the bottom of the pool. Pulled him out and tried CPR, but couldn't revive him. He was dead when the paramedics got here."

"Anyone else in the house?" I asked.

Beaton shook his head.

I rounded the pool and scanned the victim. His abbreviated Speedo revealed the tan, fit body of a man clearly in his prime. A large gash ran down his left temple below his thick dark hair.

"Secure the scene and call in the Crime Scene Unit," I told Rudy.

Beaton raised his eyebrows. "CSU? This is an accident, right?"

"We've yet to determine that. Ask the paramedics to clear their equipment and wait in the bus." I turned to Adler. "Check with the neighbors. Find out if they saw or heard anything. I'll interview the wife."

Before I approached Samantha Lovelace, I studied the scene. The narrow lap pool ran parallel to the house along the western edge of the forty-foot terrace. At the south end of the pool, a wrought-iron deck chair lay on its side. Water puddled around it. A few feet away, a pole protruded at an angle from a clump of sea oats that edged the terrace. Closer inspection revealed a long-handled skimmer net. Several feet north of the overturned chair, Lovelace's body lay in another large puddle of water, apparently where his wife had dragged him from the pool.

I stared at the beach beyond the terrace. Something was wrong with the picture and I took a moment to figure it out. A wide swath of sand, leading from the terrace between the dunes to the water's edge, had been carefully raked, like the terrain in a Japanese garden. Nothing disturbed the perfection of the white sugar-sand, no footprints, not even bird tracks, although, in the light of the rising moon, a night heron skittered through the breakers farther up the beach. Several different-size feet had made deep impressions in the sand on either side of the raked area where people had walked the shoreline before the intervening sand had been smoothed. To the west stretched the seemingly unending expanse of the Gulf of Mexico, reflecting a swath of silver moonlight. The scene was peaceful and serene.

Except for the dead body on the pool deck beside me.

"What have we got?"

I jumped at the sudden voice at my elbow. Doris Cline, wearing her usual running shoes, had sneaked up on me. For someone who'd been called out on a holiday, she looked unusually perky, more like a gung-ho, high school, physical education teacher with her bouncy gray curls, wide smile and bright eyes, than a medical examiner.

"You'll have a dead detective if you keep scaring me like that. Sorry to ruin your Thanksgiving."

Doc nodded toward the body on the pool deck. "Mine's not half as ruined as his. What happened?"

I walked her through the scenario I'd garnered from the evidence. "Here, at this first puddle, Lovelace's head somehow came in contact with that overturned wrought-iron chair. There's blood on the metal arm. Then he went into the water. His wife claims she found him in the pool, dragged him out and tried CPR."

Doc knelt on the flagstone decking, poked a finger into the first puddle of water and lifted it to her mouth. I shuddered at the gesture, but figured clear water was the least gross of the fluids Doc had to deal with.

She lifted her eyebrows. "Salt. Was he swimming in the Gulf first?"

"Not unless he raked the beach behind him when he came out, and there's no rake in sight."

Doc approached the body and scrutinized the victim. "Bleeding on the temple indicates he was alive when this injury was sustained. Those long scrapes on his chest, however, were post mortem. Probably occurred when he was dragged from the pool." She lifted the victim's right hand that sported a diamond the size of a walnut set in a gold band.

"The fact that he's still wearing that rock rules out robbery," I said.

Doc checked his left hand with its plain gold wedding band. "His nails on both hands are broken and the tips of his fingers are scraped."

"Signs of a struggle?"

She nodded. "As if he tried to claw his way out of the pool."

"Could he have been groggy from the blow to his head, so stunned that he couldn't pull himself out of the water?"

"I'll know more after the autopsy."

"Had he been in the water long?"

She shook her head.

The CSU team arrived. While Doc continued her examination of the body, I asked the techs to take samples of the two puddles and also water from the pool, as well as the blood from the chair arm. After requesting that they bag the skimmer net, I headed toward Samantha.

Although the day had been warm, the night breeze off the chilly Gulf waters was cold, and in her chair on the raised deck, Samantha was shivering. How much from physical discomfort and how much from emotional distress, I couldn't tell.

"Why don't we go inside where it's warmer," I suggested.

She looked up with a shell-shocked expression and recognition flitted across her deep blue eyes. "I know you."

"Maggie Skerritt." I took her arm, tugged her from the patio chair and led her into the living room.

"Margaret? Priscilla's daughter? What are you doing here?"

"I'm a detective with the Pelican Bay Police Department."

With the wooden expression of a sleepwalker, she sank into a chrome-and-leather chair beside a fireplace with a mirrored surround and tugged the blanket closer. She picked up a remote control from a side table, pointed it at the fireplace and punched a button. Flames flared from a gas log. Shaking her head, as if clearing mental fog, she asked, "Why are the police here?"

"Standard procedure whenever there's a death."

Samantha was ten years younger than I was. She'd always been a beauty and either good genes or a great plastic surgeon had preserved that youthful attractiveness into her late thirties. But with her makeup ruined by pool water and tears, her face appeared ravaged. My job was to sort out how much of that effect had been produced by genuine grief.

I glanced at a massive portrait of two towheaded little girls holding a Jack Russell terrier puppy that hung above the fireplace. Their resemblance to Samantha as a child was unmistakable.

"You have children?" I asked.

"Two daughters. Emily's sixteen. Dana's almost fifteen." Her face crumpled and fresh tears streaked her cheeks. "How am I going to tell them their father's gone?"

"Where are they?"

She glanced at a stylized clock of crystal and brass on the mantel. "Landing in Colorado. We had dinner at noon. Then they left with our neighbors, the Standifords, for a week of skiing in Aspen."

"I know this is hard, Samantha, but I need you to tell me what happened right up to the point you pulled your husband from the pool."

She inhaled a deep, shuddering breath and wiped her cheeks with the backs of her hands. "After dinner, we loaded the girls' luggage and ski equipment into the Standifords' SUV. After they left for the airport, I put away leftovers and cleaned up the kitchen."

"And your husband?"

"He was working in his study." She nodded toward a room at the south end of the house. "He's always working. We were lucky he took time to eat with us today." Her voice was hard with annoyance before she broke into fresh sobs. "That was the last meal we'll ever have as a family."

"And after that?" I prodded. I felt sympathy for her, but the quicker I completed my questions, the sooner I could leave her to her grief.

She wiped her nose with a corner of the blanket, a rough utilitarian item provided by the paramedics. "Vince was still working. I felt a migraine coming on, so I took my medication and went upstairs to take a nap."

"How long did you sleep?"

Her eyes, filled with agony, gazed up at me. "It was my fault, wasn't it?"

"Why do you say that?"

"If I hadn't been asleep, I might have found him in time to save him."

"Had your husband been drinking?"

She gave a short laugh, more like a hiccup. "Not a chance. He's a fitness addict. Never touches alcohol or red meat."

"Did he have an illness or take medication that might have made him dizzy and caused him to fall?"

She shook her head. "Vince just had a physical. His doctor told him he has the body of a twenty-year-old."

And now Vince Lovelace would be forever young. "Did your husband swim every day?"

"Like clockwork." The edge returned to her voice. "He always swims laps in the pool every evening before dinner. If he'd shown the same diligence toward his family...."

Trouble in paradise, but discord didn't necessarily generate foul play. "Did your husband have enemies?"

Her eyes widened with surprise. "You don't think... This was an accident, wasn't it?"

"We have to consider all possibilities. Do you know of anyone who would want to harm your husband?"

Her full lips twisted in a wry expression. "You don't reach the pinnacle of success that Vince did without stepping on a lot of people on the way up. Plenty of people hated his guts."

"Anyone in particular?"

Her answer was instantaneous. "Dan Rankin, his ex-partner."

"Bad blood?"

Samantha nodded. "Vince bought him out, right before Your Vacation Channel went big. Dan's blamed Vince for cheating him out of a fortune ever since."

"Anyone else?"

"Probably tons of people at work. You should ask his secretary. He spent more time with her than he did with me."

"Was your husband having an affair?" Hell has no fury like a woman scorned, and if Vince had been struck down in a jealous rage, he wouldn't be the first spouse murdered in a fit of passion.

"With Elaine?" Her lips lifted in an almost smile. "Elaine's old enough to be his mother and ugly as homemade sin. But she's the world's best administrative assistant."

In spite of the heat blasting from the gas logs, Samantha's shivering was accelerating.

"You'd better get out of those wet clothes," I said. "Is there anyone you can call to be with you?"

She stood on shaky legs. "My mother. And I'll have to contact the Standifords and ask them to send the girls home."

"I'm sorry for your loss, Samantha."

She nodded numbly and headed for the stairs.

As she disappeared around the landing, Adler came in through the front door.

"Neighbors to the north aren't home," he said.

"The Standifords. They're in Colorado."

"The people across the street saw nothing, heard nothing."

"You're saving the best for last, right?"

He nodded. "Neighbors to the south, the Marlowes, heard the Lovelaces screaming at each other about an hour and a half before the 911 call. Said the exchange lasted for over fifteen minutes."

"Could they hear what the argument was about?"

Adler shook his head. "But they did say it wasn't

unusual. Happened all the time over the past few months."

"People who live in glass houses should keep their windows closed. The Marlowes have any idea what the Lovelaces fought over?"

"Nope. Said the fights were always private. In public, they were a model couple."

I thought for a moment. "Samantha said Vince was in his study before his swim. It's on the south side of the house." I crossed to the doorway and peered into a den furnished with the same sparse modernism as the rest of the house. "If there was a fight, it must have been strictly verbal. No sign of anything broken or disrupted."

"Someone could have cleaned up afterward," Adler said.

"I'll suggest Samantha go home with her mother. We'll secure the house and cordon the grounds and beach. If Doc's autopsy rules out accidental drowning, we'll get a warrant for a search."

"Don't know if it's relevant," Adler said, "but the Marlowes also heard a few boats close to the beach late this afternoon."

"Could they identify them?"

"They didn't see them, but Mr. Marlowe said,

from the sound of it, at least one was high-powered, like a ski or cigarette boat."

"Nothing suspicious there. It's a holiday. Lots of people on the water."

"If I was planning a crime, I'd want a boat with powerful engines that was in and out fast." He gazed past me to the body by the pool. "You think it's a homicide?"

I shook my head. "We had three last month. Odds are it'll be years before Pelican Bay sees another murder."

I didn't tell him my skin was itching. With my allergy to homicide, if Doc's autopsy turned up evidence of foul play, by this time tomorrow, I'd have a full-blown case of hives.

It was almost midnight when I returned to my condo. Bill's car was parked out front and lights shone from my downstairs windows. Bill was the only person with a key to my place, and, tired as I was, I was glad he was there. Wired from the adrenaline rush of the investigation, I wouldn't be able to sleep for hours.

He met me at the front door. "Tough night?"

I managed a smile. "Probably no worse than if

I'd spent the entire evening in the bosom of my family."

"That bad, eh?"

I kicked off my shoes and turned toward the kitchen to make coffee. Bill grasped my shoulders, corrected my course and steered me toward the living room and into my favorite chair.

"I have to say," Bill said, his expression serious, "that I liked your family."

"You like everybody. With the exception of some particularly nasty criminals, of course."

"Your mother's not what I expected."

"She isn't?" I was amazed. As often as I'd talked about her, I figured he'd have had a pretty clear picture of the old girl.

"She's controlling, as you've said. But underneath, I don't think she's very secure."

"The Queen Mother? Insecure? Have you been drinking?"

"Not since before dinner," he said. "Bet you haven't eaten."

"Nope." My stomach growled in response. "But I'm out of luck. There's not even a Diet Coke in my fridge."

"Guess again. Estelle stopped me as I was going for my car earlier. Said to come back to the house after I dropped you off and go around to the kitchen door. When I returned, she'd packed a hamper with an entire meal for the two of us. Won't take but a minute to heat it in the microwave."

A lump formed in my throat. Estelle, bless her, worried about me. My mother, on the other hand, only fretted over the fact that I'd spoiled her perfect dinner party.

An hour later, sated with a good meal and two glasses of excellent wine, I returned to my chair in the living room.

"Tell me about Your Vacation Channel." I knew that Bill, who loved to travel, would have the lowdown on Vincent Lovelace's cable network.

Bill sat in the chair opposite me. "It's a shopping channel that sells anything and everything related to vacations. Hotel reservations, package tours, time shares, leisure wear, sports equipment."

"People actually buy that stuff off TV?" As much as I hated to shop, I couldn't imagine plunking down serious money on anything hawked on television.

"The marketing's remarkable. Your Vacation Channel doesn't just sell a ski vacation package, for example. They air documentaries that give the history of skiing, along with virtual tours of the rooms and amenities at the resorts and trips into the surrounding countryside. They show the chefs preparing the foods in the restaurants. And they present programs that teach the basics of skiing and explain how to dress for the slopes."

"Once you've watched all that, why bother going?"

He grinned. "As much as you hate to travel, you'd never understand. What you need is a Book Channel."

"What I need is some answers." Throughout dinner, the inexplicable circumstances of Vincent Lovelace's drowning had niggled at the back of my mind. I laid out the details of what I'd discovered in hopes Bill would see something I'd missed. "My instincts say he was murdered," I concluded, "but I don't have evidence to back them up."

Bill leaned forward in his chair and rolled his empty wineglass between his palms. "Could have been simply an accidental drowning. Lovelace slips on the deck, hits his head on the chair and rolls unconscious into the pool."

"Then how do you explain his broken nails and the abrasions on the tips of his fingers?"

"Maybe he didn't lose total consciousness right away. Tried to claw his way out of the pool first."

"Maybe. Or maybe someone anchored a boat off the beach, surprised Lovelace when he came out for his habitual swim, hit him with the chair and rolled him into the pool. His attacker then rakes the beach behind him to hide his tracks, returns to his boat, and sails away."

Bill thought for a moment. "As long as we're speculating, what if Mrs. Lovelace hit him with the chair, then raked the beach to make it look as if someone else had covered his tracks?"

"Motive?"

"One of the big three."

"Jealousy, greed or revenge."

He nodded.

"I need probable cause before I can get a search warrant."

"What about those fingertips?" he asked. "Defensive wounds?"

"A judge could argue they're merely signs of a drowning man's desperate struggle to get out of the water." Dinner and wine had made me drowsy, too tired to think. "I'd better get some sleep. Lovelace's autopsy is scheduled for 8:00 a.m. You want to crash on my sofa?"

"Now there's a romantic thought."

"Since when are you interested in romance?"

"You'd be surprised." He stood and leaned over to kiss me. With a lingering caress, he cupped my cheek in his big hand. "I'll let myself out."

"Bill?"

He stopped and looked at me with what appeared hopeful anticipation, but the light was low and I couldn't really tell.

"I'm sorry about tonight, your missing dinner and all."

His fleeting look of disappointment was quickly covered by a smile. "I had an excellent dinner, a little late granted, but with the one person I wanted to spend Thanksgiving."

He locked the door behind him as he left and I climbed the stairs to my bedroom, wondering why I felt so euphoric with a possible murder investigation facing me in the morning.

CHAPTER 5

Adler met me at the medical examiner's office, but he wasn't his usual cocky self. He'd endured the first three autopsies of his career during our last multiple-murder investigation, but the indignities of the procedure hadn't sat well with him. This morning, even before we entered the room, he looked green around the gills. The one consolation was that the building's air-conditioning had been repaired since the last time we were there.

Doc, humming a Bette Midler tune and looking professional but cheery in her scrubs, glanced up from the body on the stainless-steel table when we entered and pointed toward a cabinet door. "Bucket's in there, Adler."

"Thanks." Adler, who had an unfortunate propensity toward tossing his cookies during the procedure, removed a stainless-steel pail from the cabinet before joining me on the opposite side of the table from Doc.

"Just be glad," she said, "that our drowning victim isn't a floater. I had a body once that had been in the Gulf for three weeks. What the fish hadn't eaten was bloated beyond—"

"Lovelace?" I asked, taking pity on Adler, who was swallowing hard.

"Pity," Doc said. "Fine specimen of a man. Appears to have been in the peak of health. Let's see what we can find."

With clinical precision, she described his external injuries for the tape recorder. Then, with one quick snip, she removed the miniscule Speedo. Adler made it through the Y-incision, for once, without losing his stomach contents.

"You're getting better at this," I said to him.

He shook his head. "I've learned not to eat beforehand, but I'm fighting dry heaves."

The autopsy progressed and Doc's examination of Lovelace's brain ruled out a killing blow. "Enough damage here to stun him, but he was alive when he went into the pool. Water in the lungs confirms that."

With the internal organs examined, weighed and cataloged, the autopsy was over, but Doc's findings had provided nothing to conclude the drowning was anything other than accidental. The broken nails and abraded fingertips were most likely caused by the stunned man's futile efforts to climb from the pool.

Adler and I headed for the door.

"Whoa!" Doc called. "Look at this. It wasn't here earlier."

We turned back to the autopsy table where Doc had rolled the body facedown. She pointed to a round bruise, slightly smaller than a baseball, between the shoulder blades.

"How did we miss this?" I asked.

"Bruises don't always show up right away," she explained. "I've had morticians call to report bruises that didn't appear until the body was being embalmed."

"Is it a result of the autopsy?" Adler asked.

Doc shook her head. "The injury could have occurred just prior to death and only now showed up."

My mind whirled, making connections. The entire lap pool had a five-foot depth. I recalled the long-handled telescoping pole of the skimmer net, its diameter consistent with the bruise in the middle of Lovelace's back.

"When Lovelace went into the pool," I said, "somebody made damned sure he stayed under.

They held him down with the handle of the skimmer net."

Adler's gaze met mine across the table. "I'll get a search warrant for Lovelace's house and business."

"I'll meet you at the house. I have some questions for Mrs. Lovelace first."

But before that, I'd make a quick stop at the drug store for Benadryl. With a confirmed homicide, a bad case of hives wasn't far behind.

Isabelle Weston, Samantha's mother, lived on the Belle Terre waterfront street three houses down from my childhood home, a four-minute drive from the pharmacy. Unlike Mother's tile-and-stucco Misner Mediterranean, the Weston home was a rambling arts-and-craft structure of huge stones, exotic woods and wide windows, designed by a contemporary of Frank Lloyd Wright. In my youth, I'd visited the house many times with my mother, usually in connection with some charity event Isabelle and Mother had cochaired. In the past, Isabelle had always welcomed me. Under today's circumstances, I doubted she'd be pleased to see me.

A young African-American maid in a sky-blue

polyester uniform opened the door and, impressed by my detective's shield, immediately ushered me through the house to the rear deck that cantilevered over the water. Across St. Joseph Sound, the high-rises of Pelican Beach shimmered in the late-morning sun, while live oaks and massive camphor trees shaded the deck.

Isabelle, dressed in designer workout clothes, was riding a stationary bicycle as frantically as if being chased by a vicious dog. Unlike my mother, who had never worked up a sweat in her life, Isabelle thrived on physical activity and was an avid golfer and sailor. Apparently her age, about ten years younger than Mother, hadn't slowed her down. A petite woman with short, gray curls, she'd make a perfect model for AARP recruiting posters. When she caught sight of me, her brilliant hazel eyes widened with surprise.

"Margaret Skerritt! I haven't seen you in years. How are you, dear?" She ceased her frenzied pedaling, slid from the bicycle seat and grabbed a towel from the deck railing. She motioned me toward a teak chair. "Twanya, bring us iced tea, please."

Twanya nodded and returned to the house.

"Sorry, Mrs. Weston," I said, "but this isn't a social call. I have to speak with Samantha."

Isabelle shook her head. "Not possible."

"She isn't here?"

Isabelle, her face pink with exertion, plopped into a deck chair beside me and dabbed her neck and forehead with the towel. "She's still in bed. She was so upset last night, I had to call Dr. Fellows to sedate her. I'm letting her sleep, since the girls won't return from Colorado until this afternoon." Her lower lip trembled and she shook her head. "It's terrible, losing a husband and father, especially so unexpectedly. I don't know how my babies are going to cope. What a horrible accident."

I always hated this part. "It wasn't an accident."

"I'll help them all I can, of course—" She stopped midsentence as my words registered. "What do you mean, it wasn't an accident?"

"I've just come from the autopsy. Someone made certain that Vincent drowned."

"You can't be serious."

"I never joke about murder."

Her little mouth gaped, like a fish out of water. When she caught her breath, she said, "Who would have wanted to kill Vince?"

"That's what I'm trying to find out. And why I have to talk to Samantha."

She bristled as all her maternal instincts sprang into play. "Surely you don't think Samantha had anything to do with his death?"

"Samantha was closer to him than anyone. What she knows is key to my investigation."

Isabelle's fists knotted around the towel until her knuckles whitened, and her jaw set in a hard line. "That boy. As if he didn't cause enough grief when he was alive."

"What kind of grief?" I pumped as much sympathy as I could into my tone in an effort to keep her talking.

Isabelle shook her head. "He was a total workaholic. Never spent the time with Samantha or the girls that he should have. He was always chasing the almighty dollar." Isabelle's anger at her son-in-law deepened the pink in her cheeks. "Samantha pleaded with him, for the girls' sake if not for hers, to go to counseling so he could learn to slow down. He refused. Said he had to get his business on a firm footing before he could slack off. Otherwise, he was convinced he'd lose everything."

"In the end, he did."

The old woman's eyes brimmed with tears. "At

least he cared enough about his family to see that they are taken care of. We can thank Hunt for that."

"My brother-in-law?"

Isabelle nodded. "Just last month, Hunt persuaded Vince to double his life insurance. Thank God, he did. Now, although they've lost a husband and father, my girls won't lose their home and way of life."

"Isabelle?" A familiar voice rang out inside the house, followed by my mother's entry onto the deck. With every snowy hair in place and dressed in tailored camel-colored slacks, a creamy ivory twin set and her best pearls, she carried a large wicker basket looped over her arm. "I'm so sorry about Vince. I had Estelle prepare a chicken casserole and her orange chiffon cake. And if there's anything else you need, darling, you have only to ask."

Isabelle rose, greeted my mother with kisses on both cheeks, and handed the basket to Twanya, who was hovering nearby. "That's so kind of you, dear. Where would we be in times of tragedy without our friends? Add another glass to the tea tray, Twanya."

Only then did Mother notice my presence.

"Why, Margaret, I didn't expect to find you here, but I'm glad you've come to express your sympathy." For once her expression was approving.

"She's here to question Samantha," Isabelle said in a cold voice, shattering Mother's misconception of my social graces.

Mother's eyes narrowed. "Can't you leave that poor girl alone? She just lost her husband."

No one could put me on the defensive better than my mother, but I fought the urge to turn tail and run. "Vincent Lovelace wasn't lost. He was murdered. I need to talk with Samantha."

"You can wait until after the funeral," Mother said in her dismissive tone that indicated, as far as she was concerned, the matter was closed.

I took a deep breath, exhaled, and restrained myself from scratching the welts that had risen on my forearms. Although I'd taken Benadryl in the car, the antihistamine hadn't had time to take effect. "I can either talk to Samantha here or I can send a couple of uniforms to escort her to the station. What's it going to be?"

With a sigh of exasperation, Isabelle tossed aside her towel. "Samantha has nothing to hide. Let's get this over with so she can grieve in peace."

Isabelle went into the house and Mother turned

on me, her eyes flashing with fury. "Isabelle Weston is my dearest friend. How dare you cause such a scene in her home?"

Feeling five years old again, I held my ground. "I'm doing my job, Mother. Your dearest friend's son-in-law has been murdered. Don't you want his killer brought to justice?"

"Why question Samantha? Is she a suspect?"

Was my mother really such an innocent that she didn't know a spouse was at the top of the list in a murder investigation? "If Samantha is innocent, she has nothing to fear from my questions."

"I won't stay and be a party to this," Mother said with an indignant sniff, and turned her back on me. She strode across the deck and met Isabelle and Samantha coming out.

Mother hugged Samantha with more warmth than she'd ever exhibited toward me, then squeezed Isabelle's hands. "Call me if you need me."

"I'll see you to the door," Isabelle said, and the two left me alone with Samantha.

She shuffled toward a chair at the edge of the deck as if still feeling the effects of whatever drug Dr. Fellows had given her. She wore a gown and peignoir in a sheer cotton, pin-tucked, smocked and trimmed with delicate lace, an elegant contrast to the oversize departmental T-shirt I usually slept in. In spite of her sedation, her face appeared more ravaged than it had the night before, and her eyes reflected the torture of the damned, making me wonder if grief, guilt or an overdose of both caused her torment.

"I thought I'd answered all your questions last night," she said with a slight slur to her words, as if she wasn't fully awake.

"That was before we learned your husband's drowning wasn't accidental."

"What?" Her head snapped up, her eyes focused and her surprise was either genuine or a remarkable performance. "That's not possible. No one else was there."

"Except you?"

Samantha burst into tears. "I loved my husband. I can't believe anyone would think I'd...I can't even say it, much less do it!" She wiped her cheeks with the sleeve of her peignoir and glared at me. "Why would I want to harm the person I love most in the whole world?"

I felt sorry for her, but I couldn't allow sympathy to color my objectivity or temper my questions. "Who's the beneficiary on his insurance policy?"

She flinched as if I'd slapped her. "That's none of your business."

"Money's a strong motive for murder."

"Vince made tons of money. I had more than I needed."

"Your own account?"

She hesitated, then shook her head. "Vince controlled the finances, but he never denied me anything I asked for." Her tears flowed again, raining in splotches on her expensive robe. "He was a wonderful, generous man. And now he's gone."

"Your mother says he spent too much time working." I was picking up strange vibes from Samantha, genuine grief over her husband's death accompanied by distinct undertones of guilt.

She nodded. "I wanted him to spend more time with me, with our daughters." Her face crumpled. "I wanted to see more of him, and now he's gone forever."

Sensing Samantha knew more than she was telling, I prodded further. "Did you see or hear anything before you found him in the pool?"

She grew still for a moment. "Something woke me up. A boat with a loud engine. That's when I went looking for Vince. When he wasn't in his study, I checked the pool. But I didn't see him at first, because he was on the bottom. If I'd found him sooner—"

She burst into fresh sobs.

"You should leave now." Isabelle spoke behind me. "If you want to talk to Samantha again, you'll have to wait until her lawyer's present."

Isabelle's late husband had headed Pelican Bay's most prestigious law firm, so his widow knew enough law to be dangerous. The feisty little woman pushed up the sleeves of her workout jacket, as if ready, all four foot ten of her, to toss me out.

Once she'd uttered the L-word, I knew further questioning was futile.

Twanya appeared, carrying a tray with four glasses and a pitcher of tea.

"You can show Detective Skerritt out," Isabelle told her.

I rose from my chair. Samantha, still crying, buried her face in her hands. Isabelle fixed me with a lethal stare that hastened my departure.

Twanya set down her tray and escorted me to the door. As she let me out, she leaned forward and whispered, "Lady, you really know how to piss people off. I never seen Miss Isabelle so mad."

"Special course in detective school," I said with a straight face. "I aced it."

I stepped outside and sighed as the door closed behind me. With Samantha my prime suspect, between Isabelle and my mother, my butt was toast.

CHAPTER 6

I stopped at Scallops, a downtown sidewalk café, and ordered sandwiches and sodas to go before I drove across the causeway to the beach. Adler met me at the Lovelace house, warrant in hand.

We circled the house to the pool. With the patio furniture covered with fingerprint powder, we sat on the stone wall of the terrace in the sun. Adler dug into his sandwich and bag of chips with his usual gusto, but my appetite had been ruined by the run-in with my mother. I described the encounter for Adler along with what little I'd gleaned from my brief interview with Samantha.

"The only bright side of this whole scenario," I said, "is that the chief is on vacation until the beginning of next week. As long as he's in Jackson Hole, he won't be breathing down our necks."

The name of Shelton's getaway destination had the entire department vying for who could come up with the best play on words. So far, Lenny Jacobs in vice was the frontrunner with, "One good hole deserves another."

"Don't count on the chief's not knowing," Adler said. "The cable news channels were announcing Lovelace's death this morning. Heard it while I was dressing for work."

"At that time, we weren't aware that he was murdered, so the chief doesn't know yet, either."

"While I was waiting for the warrant, I ordered the logs for the house phones and the Lovelaces' cells," Adler said. "We should have a record of their recent calls by Monday."

"Monday? Why so long?"

"Holiday weekend."

If I used my imagination, I could almost pretend I was on holiday. The day was cloudless, the Gulf had barely a light chop and the white sugar-sand sparkled in the sunlight. Sea oats and palm fronds waved in the breeze, and the Lovelace house with its terraced landscaping and pool appeared as impressive by the light of day as it had in the moonlight.

Adler glanced around. "Why did someone want him dead?"

"Maybe he had something he shouldn't have. Or something someone else wanted. That's what we're here to find out." I stuffed my half-eaten sandwich into the bag and drained the last of my Diet Coke. "Any word from the crime lab?"

"Rafferty called." Adler cocked his head back to catch the crumbs from his chip bag. "Said with this case and another homicide in St. Pete, he'll have to put off processing the surveillance video you sent until sometime next week."

"Anything turn up from this crime scene?"

"No prints on the skimmer pole, but it did have Lovelace's skin cells in the crevices of the grip on the end of the handle, just as you suspected. Blood on the arm of the chair is the vic's. The first puddle of water from the pool deck tested as Gulf water. The second came from the pool."

I turned and studied the expanse of sand between the dunes. Apparently late yesterday afternoon someone had approached from the beach. A large fiddler fig by the edge of the terrace could have provided cover until Lovelace came out of the house for his regular-as-clockwork swim. The intruder must have dripped salt water onto the pool deck while he—or she—held Lovelace under after knocking him into the pool with the chair, then raked the path back to the boat to cover footprints. The sand was now riddled with bird tracks.

The crime scene tape staked across the beach into the breakers had discouraged human traffic.

"Let's look for a rake," I said.

"Wouldn't the killer have tossed it into the boat as he left?"

I nodded. "If he didn't have an accomplice who cleaned up after him."

By 4:00 p.m. Adler and I had combed every inch of the Lovelace house, grounds and garage. We found no rake or any type of gardening equipment. No pool equipment, either. Apparently the family had kept the skimmer net merely to retrieve items that fell into the pool. I did find invoices on Lovelace's desk from the lawn and pool services.

Adler took the personal computers of the victim, Samantha and her girls when he left. He would try cracking their passwords and reading their e-mails. I hoped he'd find something helpful. Our entire afternoon had turned up zip. No steamy love letters, no threatening calls on voice mail, no overt signs of marital discord, no backlog of unpaid bills or letters of extortion. All I had found of any interest was Samantha's stash of Xanax, secreted in her lingerie drawer, but whether she had a reason to feel anxious or merely had trouble sleeping, I had yet to determine.

Before leaving the Lovelace house, I called the Pelican Bay offices of Your Vacation Channel, but got only a recorded message, saying the staff would be back in the office on Monday. Adler explained that, due to the Thanksgiving weekend, all their programming was canned, requiring only a technician or two to keep the network up and running until everyone returned from vacation. I'd tried contacting Lovelace's secretary, Elaine, at home with no answer. I hoped I could track her down and Dan Rankin, the disgruntled ex-partner, before the case got any colder.

On a hunch, I stopped at the yacht club after leaving the crime scene. The sprawling bungalow-style building with its white clapboards and cypress-shingled roof hugged the dunes, its humble exterior disguising the opulence that lay inside. Only the meticulous landscaping with its well-trimmed shrubs and profusion of annuals in bloom hinted at the money needed to maintain the place.

The early-dinner crowd hadn't arrived yet and the late-lunch set had departed, so the clubhouse with its impressive old rafters, polished wooden floors, expensive floral arrangements and white linens, was almost deserted. The hatchet-faced hostess in her usual black silk dress, single-strand pearls and sour expression guarded the entrance to the dining room like a temple dog.

"Are you a member?" she asked, knowing full well I wasn't.

I tapped the shield protruding from my blazer pocket. "Detective Skerritt. I'd like to ask a few questions."

"You'll have to speak with the manager."

"That'll work."

She hurried away, her high heels tapping on the highly glossed heart-pine floors, and returned in a few minutes with a middle-aged, balding man dressed in an expensive suit and ultraconservative tie.

"I'm John Gilbert," he said. "How can I help you?"

"One of your members died yesterday, Vincent Lovelace," I began.

He nodded with sympathy. "A tragic drowning. And Mr. Lovelace such a good swimmer, too."

"What can you tell me about Mr. Lovelace?"

"I don't understand."

"Did you notice anything odd about his relationship with his family or any of the members here?"

Gilbert's expression shut down as if someone had pulled a shade. "This is a private club. What happens here stays here."

"Like Vegas?" I said with a smile, hoping to crack the sudden ice of his demeanor.

Apparently my charm factor needed work. The lines of Gilbert's face hardened. "This is private property, Detective. Unless you have a warrant, I'll have to ask you to leave."

"Thanks for your help." I glanced over his shoulder at the hostess whose smirk did nothing to soften the sharp angles of her face. "You, too. I'll be sure to tell my mother how cooperative you've been about the death of her best friend's son-in-law."

"Your mother?" Gilbert asked with a frown.

"Mrs. Philip Skerritt." Mother's attitude would be the same as the manager's, but he didn't know that.

"Oh," Gilbert said, and the hostess's smirk faded. From the distress on their faces, I could tell the Queen Mother instilled the same terror in others that she did in me, but the invocation of her name did nothing to loosen their tongues.

I restrained myself from hurrying out the door to escape the oppression I always suffered in that bastion of the elite. By the exit, an easel with a poster, decorated with gold glitter and holly leaves and berries in green-and-red velvet, caught my eye. It announced the club's annual Christmas tea to be held tomorrow afternoon. Every December Mother had invited me to attend what was one of the biggest social events of the year in Pelican Bay, and I had always refused, usually with the valid excuse that I was working. This year, I might make an exception, if only in an attempt to return to Mother's good graces after the fiasco at Isabelle's, but mainly to pick up dirt on the Lovelaces. I was that desperate to solve this case before Shelton returned.

I stepped outside, blinked in the brilliant afternoon sun, and started for my car.

"Detective?" a male voice called behind me.

I turned to see a young man, dressed in the black slacks, white shirt and black tie of the club waiter and grinding out a cigarette beneath his polished black shoe. The muscles bulging beneath his stiffly starched shirt testified that he lifted more than dinner trays. "Yes?"

"You don't know me," he said—but I recognized

him instantly. He was the waiter with buns of steel that Cedric Langford had been so enamored of the last time I'd had dinner with Mother at the club. Mother, desperate to see me married and settled, had imported Cedric from the polo grounds of Palm Beach. The old dear had been totally un- aware that the man she envisioned as a prospec- tive son-in-law was a flaming queen.

"Just wanted to say thanks for your stopping those punks a few weeks ago." The waiter's friendly enthusiasm reminded me of an overeager puppy. "The valet's a good kid. He told me the robbers wouldn't have hesitated to shoot somebody if you hadn't intervened."

"Just doing my job. Have you worked here long?"

"Couple of years."

"Can I ask you a few questions?"

He glanced back toward the clubhouse, then motioned me to a spot on the sidewalk that couldn't be seen from inside. "Anything to help a hero. What do you want to know?"

"Vince and Samantha Lovelace. They come here often?"

He shook his head. "Not the guy. But his wife's here almost every day."

"Doing what?"

"She has lunch in the sports room before her tennis lessons."

"She plays a lot of tennis?"

He shook his head. "That's the funny part. I've never seen her play with anyone. She just takes lessons. Can't blame her, though. The new pro is a looker. I'd take a few lessons myself if he weren't so enthusiastically heterosexual."

Unlike the forbidding rooms of the clubhouse, the club's tennis courts held sweet memories. My father and I had twice won the father-daughter tournament when I was in my teens. "You think there was something going on between Mrs. Lovelace and—"

"Alberto Suarez. He's from Argentina. A real Latin lover, at least on the surface. Whether he was actually getting it on with Mrs. Lovelace, I dunno. But they definitely spent a lot of time together."

"He gives lots of lessons?"

The waiter nodded. "He's raking in the dough. Just bought a top-of-the-line ski boat."

"You've seen it?"

"Yeah, the dude comes to work in it. Docks it at the club marina."

"Where does he moor it when he's not at work?"

"At Pirate's Cove, a marina in Dunedin near the apartment complex where he lives."

"Was Alberto here yesterday?"

The waiter shook his head. "Nah, nobody signed up for tennis lessons on Thanksgiving. I didn't see Alberto all day yesterday. He was here earlier this afternoon, but he's already left for the day."

This guy was a fountain of information, so I decided to push my luck. "You ever wait tables when Mr. and Mrs. Lovelace dined together?"

"Couple of times. It was sad."

"Sad?"

"They barely spoke to each other and he always took off before the dessert course. Left her sitting alone over coffee. Didn't need to be a mind reader to tell it broke her heart."

"You're sure?"

He nodded again. "I'm sensitive to feelings. Mrs. Lovelace wanted a heck of a lot more attention than her husband was giving her."

Enter Alberto and his new boat. "Thanks, you've been a big help."

When I arrived home, my answering machine indicated two messages. The first was from my mother, reiterating her displeasure over my treatment of Samantha. The second was from Bill. He sounded as excited as a kid.

"Come over as soon as you're off work, Margaret. I have something to show you. And I'll fix you dinner."

I'd tried contacting Lovelace's secretary again and Dan Rankin and Alberto Suarez without success, so, with nowhere to go at the moment with my homicide investigation, I jumped at Bill's invitation. I didn't want to spend the evening alone with my mother's reproaches ringing in my ears. And, culinarily challenged, I'm a sucker for anyone who'll cook for me.

But first I placed a call to my sister Caroline.

"Margaret?" she answered in surprise. "Is something wrong?"

I swallowed my pride and almost choked on it. "My investigation of Vincent Lovelace's death has hurt Mother's feelings, and I want to make nice."

Dead silence greeted me on the other end of the line. Undeterred, I plunged ahead. "Will you take me as your guest to the Christmas tea at the club tomorrow?"

"You've got to be kidding."

"Is that a no?"

Caroline didn't say anything.

"How many times," I said, "have I ever asked a favor of you?"

"Face it, Margaret, you act as if you don't belong to this family. Never have since Greg died."

"I know you don't approve of me, but I'm still your sister." I didn't dare admit that I wanted to attend the tea as much to glean from the club's rumor mills about the Lovelaces and Alberto Suarez as to appease Mother. I'd face Caroline's icy disdain any day if it helped solve this case before the chief got back. "Will you help me or not?"

"Do you own a dress?"

I ignored her sarcasm and pictured the utilitarian navy number that I wore for court appearances. "No."

"You'll make Mother even angrier if you embarrass her in front of her friends." She was quiet again, but I could hear the wheels turning in her brain. She'd given in, but I would have to meet her terms. "I'll take you to Neiman Marcus first thing in the morning so we can shop."

Caroline lived to shop, and the prospect of a spending excursion made her sound downright cheerful.

I considered the time it would take to drive to

Tampa and also the depleted state of my checking account. "What about the Macy's here? Or Dillard's?"

Or better yet, JCPenney or T.J. Maxx? I tried to imagine Caroline at the last two and drew a blank.

"Oh, all right," she said, "we'll try Macy's, but you'll have to agree to keep shopping if we don't find something suitable there."

"The tea is at four o'clock. We won't have much time."

"Less than you think. I have a hair appointment at two. I can get Andre to squeeze you in, too."

A styling by Andre would cost as much as my dress. I considered adding both to my expense account, then pictured the chief's reaction. "Thanks, but no time. I'm supposed to be working tomorrow."

"I'll meet you at Macy's at ten in the morning then?"

"Thanks, Caroline. I owe you."

"You certainly do," she said in a voice exactly like Mother's and hung up.

Warm air rolled across the fifty-six-degree waters of the Gulf and created a blanket of fog that reduced visibility to almost zero. I inched my Volvo along Edgewater Drive to the Pelican Bay Marina and parked in a visitor's space. Darkness and fog obscured Bill's boat at the end of the dock, but pounding noises, muffled by the fog, emanated from that direction.

Picking my way carefully along the wet planks, I reached the *Ten-Ninety-Eight*. Bill had named his boat after the radio code for "mission completed." He had finished his tour as a police officer, but Bill was never idle. Tonight, in spite of the encompassing fog, was no exception. Judging by the sounds coming from the bow, if Bill hadn't already had a boat, I'd have sworn he was building one.

"Hello!" I shouted at the first lull in the hammering.

Bill's head appeared around the end of the cabin. "Over here."

I moved to the end of the catwalk opposite the bow. Bill hopped off the boat, gave me a hug, then pointed to the front of the boat with beaming pride. "What do you think?"

At that moment, a gust of wind cleared the mist that had swirled around the bow. I blinked in surprise and words failed me. Starting at the top of the flying bridge and progressing in brightly painted wooden pairs that extended over the prow were eight prancing...flamingos?

"Well?" he prompted.

Still stunned, I was finally able to speak. "I think you have way too much time on your hands."

"Aw, Margaret." He practically deflated before my eyes. "I really hoped you'd like it."

I felt bad that I'd burst his bubble. "Maybe I'll like it better if you tell me what it is."

"The Christmas Boat Parade is Sunday night," he said, as if that explained everything.

"You've never entered before."

"I decided this year we should have some fun."

"We?"

"I need your help to pull this off."

"I'm in the middle of a homicide investigation!"

"All the more reason for some comic relief."

I eyed the bigger-than-life flamingo flock that glowed neon-salmon, even in the fog. "You got the comic part right."

"Wait right there," Bill said with all the excitement of a kid at Christmas. "You can't get the full effect without the lights."

"I don't know if my heart can take the full effect."

He grasped me by the shoulders, planted a sloppy kiss on my lips and gave me the smile that never failed to make my knees weak. "Lighten up, Margaret. I'm going to teach you how to have fun again."

He released me as suddenly as he had grabbed me, scampered back onto the boat with the agility of a much younger man and disappeared behind the cabin.

"Ready?" His voice floated to me on the fog.

"Ready," I said without much conviction, since I had no idea what I was supposed to be ready for.

Blinding light flooded the boat, surprising me so much that I stepped backward and would have gone off the dock if I hadn't grabbed a piling.

The flying bridge, ablaze in white twinkle lights, rose above me, transformed into a bamboo Santa's sleigh, whose reins, illuminated by more strings of lights, harnessed the eight flamingos, lighted by spotlights. On both the bridge and the bow, stood stylized palm trees of painted plywood with twinkle lights outlining each frond. Once on the water, away from the glow of marina lights, the bulk of Bill's boat would disappear, leaving the illusion of Santa's sleigh, pulled by the gawky birds, skimming the dark waters of the sound.

Bill reappeared on the deck in front of me and offered me his hand to tug me onboard. "What do you think?"

I thought he'd taken tackiness to new heights, but I managed to restrain myself. "I've never seen anything like it. It's remarkable."

"It is, isn't it?" He looked immensely pleased with himself and took my words as praise.

"How did you do…this?" I asked.

"I made everything in Fernandez's wood shop."

"Fernandez has a wood shop?" Fernandez, a former Tampa detective, had taken early retirement several years ago, claiming the victims of his homicide cases haunted him. Literally.

"His therapist thought a hobby would help with his problem," Bill explained. "This display is nothing compared to what Fernandez built for his own front yard. He did the entire North Pole, Santa's workshop and all."

I shuddered at the thought.

"Come inside," Bill said. "There's more."

"You've decorated inside, too?"

He shook his head and pulled me along the deck toward the sliding-glass doors at the stern.

Bracing myself for the worst, I stepped inside. But the tiny cabin looked the same as always, compact and shipshape. Not a single pink flamingo or twinkle light in sight.

"Help yourself to a beer," he said. "I'll be right back."

Bill hurried through the galley to the sleeping area. I removed a bottle of beer from the counter-size refrigerator and listened to him opening and closing cabinets and rustling tissue paper.

Frustrated and exhausted by the lack of progress in the Lovelace case, not to mention my elusive rooftop burglars, I sank onto the love seat, kicked off my shoes and propped my feet on the wicker chest that served as a coffee table.

I took a long pull on the Michelob.

"Well," Bill spoke from the galley, "what do you think?"

One look and I spewed beer all over my toes.

A Jimmy Buffett version of Santa had taken over Bill's body. He wore red Bermuda shorts, red flip-flops, a red-and-white oversize Hawaiian shirt to accommodate his pillowed paunch and a Santa hat. Most remarkable of all, however, was the flowing white beard that matched his thick hair. And sunglasses.

"If you say ho-ho-ho, I'll throw this bottle at you," I said, mopping beer off my feet.

"Ah, Margaret, where's your Christmas spirit?"

"I don't know, but it's fairly obvious you must be drinking yours."

The twinkle in his eye was very Kris Kringle. "Does that mean you won't try on your costume?"

"My costume? You've got to be kidding? Besides, I'm too big for an elf."

"But you're just the right size for Mrs. Claus. A very svelte Mrs. Claus," he amended quickly before ducking back into the sleeping area.

He returned almost immediately with a large white box. "Open it."

Fearful of what I'd find, I lifted the lid and turned back the layers of tissue. The box held a muumuu in the same red-and-white Hawaiian print as his shirt.

"You like it?" he asked.

"Yeah. This will save me a shopping trip tomorrow. I can wear it to the Christmas tea at the club. I've always wanted to give my mother and sister simultaneous heart attacks."

As soon as the words left my mouth I regretted them. Bill looked like someone whose favorite dog had just died.

He tugged off his hat and beard and sat across from me. "I'd really hoped you'd like this. I was

113

planning for us to ride together in the parade, then hand out candy to the kids at the marina party afterward."

Bill's generosity and concern for others were qualities that had drawn me to him years ago, and I wanted to kick myself for raining on his parade. I'd let my own troubles with my family and job consume me. Bill was right. My life cried out for some fun—and I should have been more aware of the needs of others. I stood, shook out the muumuu and held it against me.

"A perfect fit." I flashed him my warmest smile. "But there's a problem."

"What?" From his hesitancy, I could tell he was waiting for me to hit him with another zinger.

"Isn't Mrs. Claus's hair white?"

His good humor restored, Bill nodded with a broad grin. "Check the bottom of the box."

I removed a layer of tissue paper to reveal a white wig, gold-rimmed granny glasses and red flip-flops in my shoe size. I couldn't picture myself gussied up like Mrs. Santa, but I couldn't disappoint Bill, either.

"You think of everything," I said.

Ever sensitive to my feelings, he took the dress from me, returned it to the box and hugged me.

"You don't have to do this, Margaret, if it makes you uncomfortable."

I shook my head. "You're right. If we make some kids happy, it should be fun."

"That's my girl," he said. "One of the things I love about you is that you're such a good sport."

Curiosity prodded me to ask what other things he loved about me, but I decided now was not the time. I wanted to hear wonderful, romantic reasons, but not from a guy in a Santa suit.

"Besides," I continued, "compared to the getup my sister will force me to buy tomorrow, this outfit is much more my style."

"You're going shopping with Caroline?"

I knew that would get his attention. "To buy a dress for the Christmas tea tomorrow at the club."

Concern lit his blue eyes and he stepped back and studied my face. "Are you okay? You've always avoided that place like the plague."

"I'll just think of it as going undercover," I said and proceeded to fill him in on what I'd learned that day about the Lovelaces and Alberto Suarez.

Later Bill, now dressed in his usual attire, walked me to my car. He pointed to the box beneath my arm. "You're sure about this?"

"Of course," I lied. A died-in-the-wool introvert, I hated anything that called attention to myself, and the fact that I was willing to take part in Bill's Christmas charade was a testament to how much he meant to me. Playing Mrs. Claus would be out of character and uncomfortable, but if it made Bill happy, I'd endure it with a smile.

"Will I see you tomorrow?" he asked.

"Depends on how my investigation unfolds. What time should I be here Sunday?"

"No later than four o'clock. The boats gather at Island Estates in Clearwater, then cruise north after dark along the Intracoastal to the marina park here for the children's party."

He wrapped his arms around me and kissed me, crushing the box that held my costume. "Sleep tight, Margaret."

Already missing the warmth of his embrace, I climbed into my car and drove away. In the rearview mirror, I saw Bill watch me until I rounded a corner and lost sight of him.

Tonight I'd had a rare glimpse of another facet of Bill, a boyish, playful aspect that stood in sharp contrast to the hard-core ex-cop with his brilliant analytical mind and zero tolerance of crime. Although I had a hard time relating to his love of fun, deep down, I knew he was good for me. The sixty-four-thousand-dollar question remained.

Was I, with my workaholic tendencies and alienated family, good for him?

CHAPTER 7

At seven o'clock the next morning, I stood on the dock at Pirate's Cove Marina in Dunedin, megacup of Dunkin' Donuts' coffee in hand, and watched the sun rise over the palms, pines and acres of zoysia of the golf course at the Dunedin Country Club. With all the golf courses, marinas, beaches, parks and other tourist attractions in the county, you might guess that nobody worked in this retirement area of Florida—until you tried to travel any main road, especially during rush hour. In spite of the holiday weekend and early hour, I'd had to fight gridlock between here and the coffee shop.

I figured, even on the Saturday after Thanksgiving, Alberto would punch in at the yacht club. Too many members would be spending their weekend there for him to take the day off. If he didn't show up soon, however, I knew where he lived, just a block away, and I'd pay him a visit.

Meanwhile, I wandered the docks at the small marina, checking out ski boats. I found only three, all with names emblazoned on their sterns. I ruled out *My Children's Inheritance* and *Cheeseburger in Paradise* and focused on *Grand Slam*, as good a name as any for a tennis pro's watercraft. Obviously new, the boat's sleek lines indicated high cost and excessive power and speed. And at today's prices, Alberto had to spend a small fortune just to gas it up. I made a mental note to check into how much money tennis pros raked in. I'd already learned from the marina attendant that the monthly docking fees were more than the mortgages on some homes.

I stepped onto the catwalk that ran alongside the *Grand Slam* and knelt to study the boat's interior. Alberto had to be a neat freak, because the only items visible were the spanking-clean cushions on the seats. No sign of a rake, not even a grain of beach sand.

"What the hell are you doing?" someone shouted at me.

I stood and watched an athletic young man approach, his face red and scowling. If this was Alberto, Samantha was robbing the cradle, because if the guy was over twenty-five, I'd eat my Christmas muumuu.

"Admiring your boat," I said.

"It's private property."

"So it is. And I'm not on it. Are you Alberto Suarez?"

My question was strictly conversational. Judging by his deep tan, white shirt and shorts, expensive top-of-the-line tennis shoes and the bag of rackets he carried, he was my man.

"Who wants to know?" His dark eyes squinted with suspicion. He was handsome in a dark, swarthy way, but his eyes were too small for my taste. His build, however, reflected long hours of physical training and would probably attract at least passing interest from any woman who still possessed hormones. Sun exposure had streaked his dark hair with highlights and was already beginning to weather his skin.

I showed him my shield. "Maggie Skerritt. I'm a detective with the Pelican Bay Police Department."

His lip curled with a hint of disdain. "A detective, huh? I didn't think you wanted tennis lessons."

Nor any of the other services he was rumored

to offer, but I kept that tidbit to myself. "You know Samantha Lovelace?"

"Yeah." He straightened his shoulders and appeared to preen for an instant in studly pride. "So what?"

"I'm investigating her husband's death."

"I thought he drowned."

"He did."

"Then how come you're investigating an accident?"

With his smart-ass attitude, I liked this young punk less by the minute. "What makes you think it was an accident?"

His ego deflated slightly and his dark eyes took on a hint of wariness. "They said so on television."

"You shouldn't believe everything you hear on TV."

He dropped the bag of rackets onto the dock planking and crossed his arms in a defensive posture. "So why are you talking to me?"

"I understand you and Mrs. Lovelace are… close." I was fishing here, but I often came up with prize catches that way.

He colored beneath his tan. "Hey, I may be boinking Samantha, but I had nothing to do with her husband. I don't even know the man."

"Funny how that works. Where were you Thanksgiving?"

"At home. It was my day off."

"You spent the day alone?"

"Yeah. So what?"

"Did you take your boat out?"

He paused, as if weighing his reply. He didn't seem the sharpest knife in the drawer, but he had to know I could get the answer to my question from the marina attendant.

"Yeah, I was on the water in the afternoon."

"Lots of water out there. Can you be more specific?"

"I was just cruising. Dropped anchor off Caladesi Island for a while to check out the babes on the beach, but I was home by dark."

Only a narrow pass, not deep enough for most boats, separated Caladesi Island from the northern tip of Pelican Beach where the Lovelace home was located. Racket Man could have been in and out of the Lovelace place in minutes, with no one the wiser.

"I suppose the marina attendant can verify you were docked before nightfall?" I asked.

He looked flustered. "Jake doesn't see everything."

I considered the heavy gold chain around Alberto's neck, the gold-and-stainless-steel Rolex on his wrist, and the wink of a diamond stud in his ear. The boy obviously enjoyed the finer things in life. But was he willing to kill for them?

"I hear you're from Argentina. How come you don't have an accent?"

He tossed his carryall into the boat and frowned. "What's that got to do with anything?"

"Humor me."

"I grew up in Miami, but my parents are from Argentina. What's the harm in letting the ladies think I'm from South America?"

"One lie often leads to more."

"I'm going to be late for work, and that's no lie. Are we through here?"

"One more question. Are you in love with Samantha Lovelace?"

Emotions rippled across his face. Anger? Guilt? I couldn't tell. He broke eye contact and gazed down the canal toward the sound. "My feelings toward Samantha are none of your business."

"Guess again, pal. When her husband's been murdered, everything about anyone who knows her is my business."

"You're wasting your time with me." Alberto

cast off the lines and boarded the boat. The roar of its powerful engines made further conversation impossible, so I stood and watched him maneuver the long, sleek craft out of its slip toward open water.

Alberto Suarez was no innocent, of that I was certain, but I had no evidence to prove he was a killer.

By 10:00 a.m. I was waiting at the entrance to Macy's and watching the ice skaters on the mall's central rink. I'd checked with Jake, the marina attendant, before leaving Pirate's Cove, but he hadn't witnessed Alberto's return yesterday and couldn't give me a time. He could only verify that the cigarette boat had been in its slip when he clocked out at 8:00 p.m.

Caroline was late, so I entertained myself by people watching. The mall's customers were a cross section of Pelican Bay's population. Gray-haired seniors in Bermuda shorts and sturdy Reeboks power walked their way around the rink. A few broke off at the food court, apparently anxious to replenish the calories they'd just burned. Young couples pushed baby strollers loaded not only with their offspring but enough paraphernalia for a safari.

A knot of teenage girls, belly buttons bare and navel rings flashing, walked with the swagger of mall ownership and oblivion to others. One had combed her bright green hair into spikes that gave her a disturbing resemblance to a Chia Pet. Another had a rodent tattooed on her shoulder with its thin tail wrapped around her neck. From my years of experience as a cop, I knew that adolescent rebellion took many forms. Outrageous dress was one of them, and, unfortunately, was often a first step toward even more antisocial behavior. I wondered how long before I'd run into Miss Chia or Rat Gal in an official capacity.

"Sorry, I'm late," Caroline spoke behind me, "but I couldn't do a thing with my hair this morning."

My sister never appeared in public without being impeccably attired and made up and with every hair in place. This morning, she was wearing a heather tweed skirt of muted pastels, a crisp white blouse and a dusty-pink suede blazer with matching pumps. I thought her a bit overdressed for the mall.

"Don't you have a hair salon appointment this

afternoon?" I asked. She probably cleaned house before the maid arrived, too.

She was eyeing my hair with obvious skepticism, and I recalled too late that I'd failed to run a comb through locks that had been randomly rearranged by gulf breezes since I'd left the house at 6:00 a.m.

Caroline opened her mouth and I braced myself for the usual criticism. Instead she said, "Let's get going. We don't have much time."

With me in tow, she sailed into Macy's and headed straight for the ladies' department as if she had a built-in GPS. Caroline lived to shop, and I doubted there was an upscale retail shop within a hundred miles she couldn't find with her eyes closed.

In the ladies' department, I made a beeline for the sale rack. Caroline's gasp of horror and quick course correction had me standing in front of the designer collection.

"Hold out your hands," she ordered.

With a religious zeal shining in her eyes, she picked through the rack, grimacing at this outfit, plucking another to place in my outstretched arms. Within a matter of minutes, I held enough silk, taffeta and chiffon to clothe a Miss America Pageant.

"I don't think any of these are really me," I protested from behind the mountain of garments.

"I certainly hope not," Caroline responded emphatically. "That's the whole point, isn't it?"

I had to agree. If I showed up at the Christmas tea looking like my usual self, Mother would be mortified. And with my undercover mission, I had to blend in. My usual clothes had cop written all over them.

A clerk who knew Caroline by name practically bowed and scraped all the way to the dressing room. "Right this way, Mrs. Yarborough, and if there's anything you need, just press that buzzer."

I needed a good stiff drink, but I don't think that's what the saleslady had in mind.

Feeling like a child sent to her room for punishment, I entered the changing cubicle. Caroline settled into an overstuffed chair by the three-way mirror. "I want to see each one," she ordered.

Inside the cramped space, I removed my blazer, exposing my shoulder holster with its Smith & Wesson. Knowing security monitored the room with hidden cameras, I hung my sidearm on a hook and clipped my badge conspicuously to the holster. Caroline would never forgive me for embarrassing her if I got us even temporarily detained.

Forty-five minutes later I'd tried on every dress Caroline had selected, but none, thank God, had pleased her. I wasn't the dressy type, and I had looked like an idiot in every one. You can put lipstick on a pig, but it's still a pig.

"I don't understand why none of these work," she said. "With your looks, you should be able to wear anything."

I wasn't sure how to take that. "You're the pretty one in the family."

Caroline appeared surprised. "You think so?"

"Without a doubt. You could have doubled for Grace Kelly." And she definitely had the princess thing down pat.

My compliment seemed to please her, and, for once, she smiled at me with affection. "I always thought Daddy liked you best because you look like his side of the family, hazel eyes and brown hair."

I shook my head. "Daddy adored you because you look exactly like Mother."

A quiver of insecurity flitted across her face before she composed herself with a stiffening of her shoulders. "This isn't solving the problem at hand."

The clerk, anxious to please, hovered in a corner of the dressing room and wrung her hands.

"Look," I said to saleswoman, "I'm more into tailored. Don't you have something in a dressy skirt and jacket?"

She glanced to Caroline for approval.

My sister checked her watch. "At this point, I'm willing to look at anything. I really don't have time to try another store."

"I think I have just the solution." The clerk hurried out and returned almost instantly with a taffeta tartan skirt, a cropped black velvet jacket with a round neckline and a sheer, lace-trimmed blouse.

Caroline's expression brightened. "That might work."

With a sinking heart, I donned the ensemble and walked to the mirror. The lace on the stand-up collar scratched my neck, further irritating my burgeoning hives, and the flowing lace cuffs practically covered my hands. The hem of the black jacket hugged my waist, exposing the plaid breadth of my hips for all to see.

"I look like the drum major for the Dunedin High School Scottish Band."

Caroline clasped her hands together. "It's perfect. All you need are proper stockings and shoes. And your hair and makeup done, of course."

"What, no bagpipe?"

"Oh, stop, Margaret. You really do look charming. No one will recognize you."

"You're too kind."

But she had a point. If my purpose was to eavesdrop on the latest gossip on the Lovelaces, blending in was key. And if Caroline loved my Bonnie Lassie disguise, so would Mother.

Only one hurdle remained. I glanced at the price tag and caught my breath. "Good grief, Caroline. I don't think I paid this much for my car. Isn't there a consignment shop nearby?"

"Don't be silly. You get what you pay for, and anyone can see this is quality."

All I could see was insanity, but I was desperate to solve the Lovelace case before Shelton returned from Jackson Hole. And mollifying my mother couldn't hurt, either. I bit the bullet and handed the clerk my credit card.

I had hoped the outfit was enough to satisfy Caroline, but, enjoying the rare pleasure of having me at her mercy, she stood with the smile of a cat cornering a mouse. "Next stop, shoe department."

An hour later, with my credit card halfway to maxed out and my trunk full of packages, I headed for the station to meet Adler and compare notes.

Yesterday he'd garnered some interesting info from one of the Lovelace teens' e-mails. In an instant chat exchange, Emily had written her best friend about how tired she was of her parents' bickering:

Dad's almost never home, and when he is, Mom is always on his case. Chilling's one thing, but the temperature around here is arctic! I think they hate each other.

Do you think they'll get a divorce?

I don't like to think about it, but it's possible. Mom's so miserable.

And your dad?

I never see him. When he's home, he stays in his office.

Marital bliss had definitely gone AWOL from the Lovelace house, but I had yet to discover if the situation had deteriorated to the point of violence.

Adler's task for the morning had been to track down Elaine Bassett and Dan Rankin to see what light they could shed on the murder. Adler was at his desk in CID, filling out reports, when I reached the P.D.

"Elaine Bassett lives on the south side of town," he said. "She's in her late fifties, a widow, and she was spending Thanksgiving weekend with her brother in Lakeland. She came back early when she heard about Lovelace's death on TV."

He dived into a paper bag on his blotter and pulled out a foot-long sub. "Want half?"

I shook my head. "I picked up a salad at the food court."

"Mrs. Bassett was really broken up," Adler continued. "Said she thought of Lovelace as the son she'd never had."

That comment hit too close to home, so I hurried him along. "Did she provide any leads?"

He nodded. "Once she stopped crying and pulled herself together. Lovelace had a lot of enemies."

"You make a list?"

He wiped his fingers on a paper napkin and pulled his notebook from the pocket of his leather bomber jacket. "Dan Rankin is at the top."

"Lovelace's former partner?" My hives were giving me fits. I had already downed Benadryl capsules, so I reached into my desk for backup and rubbed lotion onto my forearms. "Is Rankin still ticked because Lovelace bought him out before Your Vacation Channel went big?"

Adler nodded and fixed me with a stare. "You ever considered the irony?"

"Of Rankin's missing out on a fortune?"

Adler shook his head. "Of a homicide detective allergic to murder." He circled his face with his index finger, alerting me that my splotches had spread.

I slathered lotion on my cheeks and forehead and made a mental note to wash my face before dressing for the tea. Otherwise, I'd arrive at the yacht club looking like the queen of the zombies.

"Rankin visited Lovelace at his office the day before Thanksgiving," Adler said. "They met behind closed doors, but Mrs. Bassett could hear that they were having a knock-down-drag-out fight. Said it got so bad, she was on the verge of calling security when Rankin stormed out."

"Same old grudge?"

"Variation on a theme. Rankin needed a loan. Lovelace wouldn't give it. Rankin was royally pissed because he'd loaned Lovelace the money to start Your Vacation Channel. He expected some quid pro quo. Lovelace told him to take a hike."

"Bassett told you all this?"

"She wants Lovelace's killer caught, and she thinks Rankin's our man."

"He apparently has motive."

"Mrs. Bassett heard him threaten Lovelace as he was leaving. Said he'd see him in hell."

"Did you get Rankin's side of the story?"

"Tried, but no luck. According to his neighbors, the Rankins are in Atlanta. Won't be back until next week."

"When did they leave?"

"Early yesterday morning."

"So Rankin was in town at the time of the murder?"

"Yeah." Adler looked as pleased as a kid with a new puppy. "And you're going to love this. After talking to their neighbors, I snooped around the outside of Rankin's house. He lives on a canal in the neighborhood just south of Pelican Point."

"He has access to the water?"

Adler nodded. "Rankin owns his own dock. Where he moors his ski boat."

CHAPTER 8

The only thing worse than a murder investigation with no hot leads is a murder investigation with too many hot leads. As I dressed for the Christmas tea, I considered the plethora of suspects Mrs. Bassett had provided Adler. Not only did Rankin hate Lovelace's guts, the cable guru had a long list of disgruntled employees. But with Alberto and Rankin having motive, means and opportunity in the form of ski boats, I intended to concentrate on them—unless my undercover assignment at the yacht club guided me in another direction.

When I reached the clubhouse portico, the valet was the same one who'd been held at gunpoint by thugs a few weeks earlier when I'd intervened. He all but hugged me when I got out of my car. I'd have parked it myself, but I doubted I'd make it back across the street without breaking my neck or an ankle in the black suede stiletto heels Caroline had picked out.

The teen gave my Highland fling outfit the once-over and me a thumb's-up. "Looking good, Detective Skerritt!"

I put my finger to my lips. "Just Ms. Skerritt today, okay?"

He winked and nodded, then leaned closer and whispered in my ear, "You packing heat?"

The comfortable bulk of my Smith & Wesson nestled beneath my jacket. "Think I'll need it for this hen party?"

"You never know," he said with a shiver. "Get this many females in one room, you're asking for trouble."

I climbed the steps to the lobby, hoping to find answers, not trouble.

Mother was the first person I encountered. She was standing with the other members of her committee in a receiving line. I had to give Caroline fashion credit, because the old girl did a double take before recognizing me. With amazing quickness for a woman in her eighties, she hurried over, grabbed me by the elbow and steered me to a corner.

"What are you doing here?"

I attempted to appear innocent. "I thought you'd be glad to see me. You've been asking me to attend the Christmas tea for over twenty years. I decided to honor your request."

Her eyes narrowed. "The Lovelaces aren't here."

"Of course not, under the circumstances."

"And I don't want you questioning my friends."

I crossed my heart. "No questions, I promise."

But only because at the first hint of interrogation, the mouth of every woman in the room would close tighter than a miser's fist. I planned to be a very good listener.

"I'm aware that you're unhappy with my investigation, Mother, but I also know you want me to find Vincent Lovelace's killer and to make certain Samantha and her girls aren't in danger. I'm going to do my best, but first I wanted to do something for you."

Mother's skeptical expression didn't waver, so I kept talking. "That's why I'm here. I even splurged on a new outfit for the occasion. How do you like it?"

I tried not to wince, recognizing that behind my verbal tap dance was a pathetic need for approval.

Mother's expression softened. "It's lovely." For an instant her eyes glistened with moisture. "Sometimes you remind me so much of your father."

Dear old Dad had been too busy at his cardiology practice to indulge in cross-dressing, so I knew she referred to my physical resemblance, not my Bonnie Lassie duds. "I miss him, too."

With a self-conscious sniff and a straightening of her thin shoulders, she morphed into her former terrifying self. "Just keep a low profile, please. I don't want people…getting the wrong impression."

"I'll try not to spill anything," I promised.

With a shake of her head and the look that always made me believe she thought I was a changeling, switched at birth by evil fairies, she returned to the receiving line.

With my antimurder hives further irritated by Mother, lace and panty hose, I headed for the tea table with very careful stiletto steps. Mother would never forgive me if I tripped and dived headfirst into the eggnog. I filled a plate with canapés and cookies, found a deserted corner within earshot of the refreshment table and sat down, all ears.

Ladies from teens to eighty and dressed in finery whose cost would have supported a Third World country sauntered past. I'd attended high school with some of these women and, although I recognized a few faces, didn't recall their names. Even in my youth, much to Mother's dismay, I'd been a bookworm, not a social butterfly.

"Poor Samantha." A woman close to my age paused at the punch bowl. "How sad to be a widow so young."

With a wicked twinkle in her eye, her companion lowered her voice. "But she has Alberto to console her."

"The tennis pro? You're not serious?"

"Of course I'm serious, darling. Everyone knows she's been carrying on with him for months. They haven't been very discreet, the way they disappear into her private cabana after every tennis lesson. It's almost as if she were flaunting the fact. I wouldn't be surprised if poor Vincent drowned himself in despair."

I took a bite of a water chestnut wrapped in bacon. The media hadn't gotten hold of the fact that our vic was murdered, so that information hadn't hit print or the airways yet.

"His poor girls," the second woman said.

"Devastated, but not poor," her friend corrected. "Vince was worth a billion. My husband's his accountant."

"Isn't that information privileged?"

"Only the specifics. I'm just giving you a ballpark figure."

"Wouldn't mind playing in that ballpark myself," her friend murmured. "Don't look now, but did you see the dress Frances Bailey is wearing? It's so tight, she looks like a sausage."

I waded through a couple plates of hors d'oeuvres, some eggnog and a cup of Russian tea while listening to variations on the same theme. Samantha, it seemed, had made no effort to hide her affair with Alberto. If anything, she had played it to the hilt, making me wonder if she had been trying to make her husband jealous, just to get his attention. Isabelle had warned that I couldn't speak to Samantha again without her lawyer, so I decided to call and set up an appointment for tomorrow, giving them time to arrange for the attorney to be there during my interrogation.

On the surface, Samantha was a prime suspect, an unhappy wife with a lover on the side and a fortune to inherit, but something was wrong with the picture and I couldn't make the pieces fit. If she had whacked Vincent with a deck chair and held him under with the pool skimmer until he drowned, who had raked the beach to make it look as if the assailant had approached by boat? And where had the rake gone? If she'd tossed it into the water, it hadn't washed up on any of the nearby beaches that the crime techs had combed. Had a lovesick Alberto, wanting Samantha for himself, been her coconspirator?

I handed my empty dishes to a passing waiter and slipped out the French doors. The salt air was refreshing after the perfume-heavy atmosphere of the clubhouse, and the ping of tennis balls against rackets carried on the breeze.

I followed the neatly swept brick walkway around the clubhouse past the Olympic-size pool and a row of private cabanas to the tennis courts, conveniently fenced along the waterfront so there was no need for a water spaniel to retrieve errant balls. Alberto stood on the service line of the nearest court with his arms around a young woman in her twenties. He was allegedly demonstrating the proper grip and follow-through for her backhand, but they weren't keeping their eyes on the ball and Alberto's hold on the woman was too intimate for tennis. He was up to some other game.

The woman's throaty laugh floated on the wind and she released her two-handed grip on her racket to caress Alberto's cheek. He responded by fondling her backside and dropping a quick kiss on her upturned face.

I found their involvement interesting. Alberto apparently was playing the field and I wondered if Samantha was aware of his philandering. The fact that he was romancing at least one other woman, of course, didn't rule out his involvement in the Lovelace murder. A man with a heart black enough to kill would have no qualms about infidelity.

I stood for several more minutes, taking in the spectacle of a woman making a fool of herself and scratching the hives on my arms with blessed relief. As on Thanksgiving Day on the Lovelace terrace, something was wrong with this picture. If Alberto had conspired with Samantha to whack her husband in order to marry the widow and claim her inheritance, he was being inordinately cavalier about his involvement with another woman. Wouldn't a man who had planned such a scheme that carefully at least play the part of faithful lover until he had the cash in his hands?

I returned to the clubhouse by the same French doors and spotted Caroline across the room, laughing with a group of her friends. Eight years had separated us as children, so that we had never been close. I had always been too young to tag along, too much of a pain in the butt for Caroline and her cronies. When Caroline had married, I was only fourteen. I'd hoped that once I reached adulthood, our age difference could be breached, but after entering the police academy, I recognized that my mother and sister lived in a different world, as strange and alien to mine as the other side of the moon. They were my own blood, but my police partners were my family.

Especially Bill.

Standing amid the rich and famous of Pelican Bay, I was overcome with a longing that frightened me with its intensity. With Bill, there was no pretense. I could be myself and he accepted me, made me feel good about who I was. With Mother and Caroline, unless I played the part of society dame, I was persona non grata, an embarrassment, a disappointment.

Choking on the rarefied atmosphere, I hurried to the entrance and asked the valet to bring my car.

At home, I changed my Scottish costume for jeans and a chambray blouse before returning to the station. Shelton would return from vacation on Monday, and I was no closer to solving Vincent Lovelace's murder than I had been the day he drowned. It was going to be a long night.

I pulled out a legal pad and began drawing up a case grid. Names of suspects down the left-hand side. Columns for motive, means, opportunity and unanswered questions across the top. Samantha led the suspect list, followed by Alberto, Dan Rankin and Lovelace's disgruntled employees. At the bottom of the list I added a question mark.

The majority of murder victims are killed by people they know, but a handful are random victims, folks in the wrong place at the wrong time. I had to consider the possibility that some twisted psychopath, who hadn't known Vincent at all, had seized the opportunity to kill unobserved. The murderer could have been someone with a general grudge against the rich, a simmering hatred based on envy of all who lived as Lovelace did. If the latter were the case, without a stroke of amazing luck, I had little hope of solving the crime before Chief Shelton returned—if at all.

Footsteps in the hall announced Adler's arrival and he appeared at the door. "I thought you were going to the yacht club."

"You said you would be at your in-laws."

HOLIDAYS ARE MURDER

His face crinkled in a boyish grin. "Guess we're living proof that some things are worse than work."

He shrugged out of his bomber jacket, straddled his desk chair and booted up one of the computers we'd taken from the Lovelace house.

"Find out anything useful?" he asked.

"Maybe. Alberto Suarez and Samantha definitely had a thing going. But lover boy has a roving eye—and hands. If he plotted to kill Lovelace to clear the way to Samantha and Vince's money, he's jeopardizing his chances if Samantha finds out she's one of many."

He glanced at my grid. "You've put their names down as prime suspects."

"For now. I need to talk to Samantha again. I'll call tonight to set up a meeting tomorrow."

"A meeting?"

"With her and her lawyer."

"Right. I forgot that her old man was an attorney and a judge. You want something to eat?"

"No thanks. My stomach is still roiling from the rich food at the club."

Adler went to the break room and returned with a can of Coke and a bag of chips. He opened a computer file and started reading while I called the Weston household and asked Twanya to tell

145

Samantha that I'd meet with her and her lawyer at two o'clock tomorrow.

"Don't you want to talk to Miss Isabelle?" Twanya asked.

"No." After my afternoon at the club, I'd suffered all the rejection I could tolerate for one day. "Just have her call me at the station if she needs to change the time."

I hung up, and Adler let out a low whistle.

"What?" I asked.

"I've been studying Lovelace's Quicken files. This one lists his assets."

"I heard his accountant's wife blabbing at the club this afternoon that Lovelace was worth at least a billion."

"She got that right," Adler said, "but that's not all. The man has a ten-million-dollar insurance policy."

I thought for a moment. "If it's double indemnity and Lovelace's death had been ruled accidental drowning, someone would have received twenty-million smackers. Does that file give a beneficiary?"

Adler shook his head. "Just dollar amounts."

I glanced at my watch. Caroline was probably still at the club, supervising cleanup after the tea. "It's time I paid a call on my brother-in-law."

Adler raised his eyebrows in surprise. "Aren't you taking this family togetherness a bit far?"

"This isn't family. It's business. Hunt wrote Lovelace's policy. He knows who collects the ten million."

CHAPTER 9

Hunt and Caroline lived in the same neighborhood as Mother and Isabelle, but in a smaller house a block from the water. The sun had already set by the time I rang Hunt's doorbell and the western sky was ablaze with shades of magenta and tangerine.

Hunt answered the door. "Margaret? What's wrong?"

The fact that he considered my presence on his doorstep an indication of trouble was an interesting commentary on my status in the family.

"Nothing. I—"

"Caroline's still at the club."

"No problem. I came to see you."

"Me?" He eyed me with suspicion. "If it's about some family squabble, I refuse to get involved."

"I don't need a referee," I said, although, Lord knows, there'd been times when I could have used one. "I need facts. For the Lovelace investigation."

Hunt hesitated, ambivalence written all over

his heavy face. On the one hand, he was world class at kissing up to his mother-in-law and probably wanted no part in any association that would tick Mother off. On the other, however, was his favorite hobby. Hunt was addicted to mysteries, *Spenser* mysteries in particular. He'd read every book—several times—that Robert B. Parker had ever published, had videotapes of every televised version, and years ago had even bought a dog he'd named Pearl. He delighted when the weather chilled so he could don his worn leather jacket, jeans and running shoes for his best Spenser imitation. The only thing missing was Hawk, Spenser's intimidating sidekick. But I supposed Caroline was intimidating enough.

I understood his fascination. The man spent his days with dry actuarial tables, insurance policy legalese and spreadsheets. He needed a diversion. And now I was offering him a part in a real investigation.

He glanced at his watch. "I can only give you a few minutes. Caroline will be home soon."

Hunt's thirst for excitement had prevailed. He opened the door and motioned me toward his den. Apparently Caroline had allowed him to dress himself today. He was attired in baggy Bermuda shorts, a safari shirt and Birkenstocks with black dress socks.

He gestured toward a club chair in his paneled retreat, filled with bookcases crammed with mystery books and videos. My feet still ached from the torture of several hours in stiletto heels and I sank into the leather embrace with gratitude. Hunt sat across from me in a matching chair and crossed his legs. His exposed white shins flashed in the dim light. They were not a pretty sight.

"So," he began, "you're saying Vince was murdered?"

"I'm not saying it. The evidence does."

"It's unbelievable. Vince sat in that very chair just a few weeks ago." Hunt shook his head and reached for a crystal decanter on the table beside him. "Want a drink?"

"No, thanks." Benadryl had loaded my system with enough foreign substance for one evening. "Was that when he increased his insurance coverage?"

Hunt had poured himself a Scotch, but he suspended his glass halfway to his mouth. "How did you know?"

"I'll know everything there is to know about Vincent Lovelace before I'm through. I'm aware that he increased his life insurance to ten million dollars. Was it double indemnity?"

"Of course," Hunt said, and his nearsighted eyes widened behind his bifocals as the implication hit him. "So if his drowning had been accidental, the policy would pay out twenty million."

"My question is, to whom?"

He shifted uncomfortably in his chair. "I can't share my client's confidential information."

"Your client's dead. Someone killed him. And if it wasn't Samantha—"

"Not Samantha! Of course not." He coughed, choking on his whiskey.

"—then she and her girls may be in danger, too. I need info, Hunt, and I need it fast."

He hesitated, took another swallow and set down his glass. "I urged Vince to change the beneficiary when he upped the coverage. Until then, Vince had named his estate as beneficiary. That meant the payout from the policy would be subject to estate taxes. However, money going directly to an individual doesn't go through probate and avoids the tax."

"So who gets the ten million?"

He hesitated only momentarily. "Samantha, naturally."

"And who gets his billion-dollar estate?"

"I would assume Samantha and the girls, but you'll have to ask Ted Trask. He handled Vince's will."

"Did Lovelace have any other policies on his life?"

Hunt shook his head. "Not that I wrote." He looked at me as if I'd just crawled from under a rock. "You don't really suspect Samantha of killing her own husband?"

"You've read enough mysteries to know everyone's a suspect until the actual killer is found."

"That's how Spenser works," he agreed. His expression turned thoughtful. "Speaking of mysteries, I'm thinking of writing one myself."

"Why not?" I didn't take him seriously. In my former life as a librarian, I'd heard dozens of people claim they were going to write a book, but I couldn't remember anyone who'd actually carried out their intent.

"Would you serve as my law enforcement consultant?"

I eyed my brother-in-law with fresh interest. "You sound serious."

"I have a great idea for a plot. My protagonist is a mild-mannered insurance agent."

I tried not to yawn. "That'll have the books flying off the shelves."

Not recognizing my sarcasm, he smiled. "I'm basing the story on a real event that happened a couple decades back. An unscrupulous agent was taking out huge policies on elderly people without their knowledge and naming a church as the beneficiary."

"And he killed people so their life insurance would go to a church?"

Hunt shook his head. "There was no church. And he didn't have to kill them. They were all within years of dying of old age. The church was merely a front for the agent who faked the applications. The main character in my story is another insurance agent who uncovers the scam. What do you think?"

"You really want to besmirch your own profession with a book that has an insurance agent as the villain?"

He laughed. "Get real, Margaret. Insurance agents rank right up there with used car salesmen, the media and politicians on the who-don't-you-trust list. I doubt a book by me would drag them any lower."

An antique clock on the mantel chimed the

hour. "I should go," I said, "before Caroline gets home."

At the mention of his wife's name, he ejected from his chair like a fighter pilot with fire in the cockpit. "I'll see you out. And I'd appreciate it if you wouldn't tell Caroline or your mother that I talked to you."

"Sure," I said out loud, adding to myself, Yeah, guy, they scare me, too.

I returned to the station and was passing the dispatch desk when Darcy called my name.

"You have a visitor," she said.

"In my office?"

She shook her head and rolled her dark eyes. "In the chief's office. Councilman Ulrich."

Ulrich was the man behind the move to disband the department and the last person I wanted to see. "Did you tell him I was out?"

"He just got here. I was dialing your beeper as you came in."

I glanced around for an avenue of escape.

"Might as well get it over with," Darcy said. "Ulrich said he'd wait, no matter how long it took."

My hives were giving me fits, so I stopped at the

water fountain and popped another Benadryl before entering the chief's office. Better living through chemistry.

Ulrich stood in front of Shelton's trophy wall, hands clasped behind his back. He was reading the framed certificates and commendations.

"You wanted to see me?" I asked.

Ulrich turned and I was struck by how small he was, barely five foot three, a Napoleonic figure with thinning hair styled in a comb-over, paunchy stomach and an aura of self-importance. In his early sixties and retired from a corporate career in the automotive industry, he'd made no secret of his political aspirations. Helping the county's dominant political machine move one step closer to a metro-style government by having the sheriff's department police Pelican Bay would garner heavy clout for his move up the ladder. He had his eye on the Pelican Bay seat in the Florida senate, a mere stepping-stone to the governor's office.

He waved me toward a seat in front of the desk and settled in the chief's special ergonomic chair as if it were his own. Clasping his hands, mottled with age spots, on a file folder lying closed on the blotter, he considered me with the look of a predatory animal analyzing his prey. "I understand there's been another murder."

"Bad news travels fast."

"That's four in a matter of weeks. Not good for the department."

"Even worse for the victims." I had no idea what Ulrich wanted, but I doubted his intentions were good.

"Have you ever been the subject of a lawsuit, Detective?"

"You don't know much about police work, do you?"

"Enlighten me."

"The better a cop does his job, the more likely he is to be shot, injured, complained on, investigated, subpoenaed on his day off or sued."

"You're avoiding my question. Have you ever been sued?"

His out-of-the-blue curve ball had caught me by surprise, making me wonder if someone had filed charges I didn't know about. "No. Why?"

"No?" He opened the folder. "According to your personnel file, an action was filed against you in Tampa, claiming you used unnecessary force, resulting in the death of one Tyrone Taylor."

"That was twenty-two years ago. Taylor, who

HOLIDAYS ARE MURDER

was out of his mind on drugs, was attempting to hack my partner with a machete. The review board took the charge under advisement and I was cleared. Subsequently, Mrs. Taylor, herself the victim of Tyrone's domestic abuse, dropped the lawsuit."

Ulrich didn't blink and tapped the paper in front of him with his index finger. "Lawsuits against police officers cost the city unnecessary taxpayer dollars."

My first thought was that Isabelle Weston had taken action, but I couldn't figure what grounds she'd have for dragging me to court. Not that a lawyer needed grounds if his retainer was hefty enough. "Has there been a suit filed that I don't know about?"

"Not at the moment." Ulrich frowned. "And if we disband this department, the city will no longer have to pay to defend lawsuits against police officers, not even frivolous ones."

Noting his deadly serious expression, I stifled a laugh at his twisted logic. "You don't really believe that sheriff's deputies are never sued?"

"Of course not." His mouth curved in a feline grin. "But the county picks up the tab for their defense costs, not the city. That fact will be a major

157

element in my argument to disband this department. The city has paid over a million dollars in
attorney's fees over the last decade to defend lawsuits against its police officers. I intend to stop the
fiscal bleeding."

My mouth gaped, and I shut it quickly. "Who
do you think pays to defend sheriff's deputies? The
Tooth Fairy?"

"County legal fees are not my problem."

"The people of this city aren't stupid. They'll
figure out that what they save in city taxes by disbanding the department will eventually come out
of their other pocket in increased county assess-
ments."

"Again, not my problem. I will have saved them
money, and they will rise up and call me blessed.
Any wrath over county taxes will be aimed at
county commissioners, not me."

"This is all about you and your political am-
bitions, isn't it?" Anger loosened my tongue and
I plunged ahead, oblivious to consequences. "I've
done the math, Councilman. By disbanding this
department, you'll save most citizens on their
city taxes slightly less per year than the price of
a dinner for two in a good restaurant. Initially.
Within a few years, the subsequent increase in

county taxes will far override that. And Pelican Bay will lose control over their own police force and suffer a reduction in services. Your proposal will also cost a lot of good men and women their jobs. All for the sake of your political aspirations."

If my accusations affected him, he didn't show it. "What about your own aspirations?"

"This isn't about me."

"But it is. That's why I wanted to see you. You're a native of Pelican Bay. Your father was a very influential man and your mother is highly respected. If you endorse disbanding the department, people will listen."

"Haven't you heard a word I've said?" I shook my head in disgust. "Why would I endorse something I know is wrong?"

"For what's in it for you."

"There's nothing in it for me!"

He reached for the chief's letter opener, a pewter replica of a Vietnam-era rifle with bayonet fixed, and pointed it at me. "You could be a lieutenant in the sheriff's CID."

"That sounds like a bribe."

"It's a political reality. One hand washes the other."

I stood to end the discussion. "Both your hands are dirty. I want no part of this."

I was halfway to the door when he spoke again. "Not you, perhaps, but someone else will. And, Detective."

I turned and glared at him. "What?"

"If you're not with me, you're against me. Just remember, I have powerful friends—and a long memory."

"Neither of which will help you sleep at night or enable you to face yourself in the mirror." I left the office and slammed the door behind me.

Darcy took one look at my face. "You okay?"

Feeling as if I'd rolled in slime, I stomped down the hall toward my office. "Nothing a good hot shower and a barrel of disinfectant won't cure."

I slept late Sunday morning and had to scurry to meet Samantha at the law offices of Weston, Dykeman and Bertelli, a Tudor-style complex of brick and dark timbers nestled beneath moss-draped live oaks at the east end of Main Street. Samantha had left a message on my answering machine the previous night, saying her lawyer, Harvey Dykeman, could meet with us at noon.

When I arrived, Dykeman himself opened the

door. The tall, thin man, who had an amusing resemblance to a great blue heron with his gangly arms and legs and custom-made blue suit, ushered me into the conference room where Samantha sat. Isabelle, thank goodness, was nowhere in sight.

Samantha looked as if she'd been dragged through a knothole. Her hair, still damp from a shower, was slicked back from a face devoid of makeup, and her slacks and blouse were uncoordinated. The woman's distressed appearance could have been her actual state or a defense ploy.

She startled me by asking Dykeman to leave us alone.

"You need representation, Samantha," the elderly lawyer insisted. "Talking to the police without your attorney is unwise, even dangerous."

She lifted her head and met his gaze. "I have nothing to hide."

He shook his head. "That won't keep them from charging you with Vince's murder."

"At this point, I don't give a damn." Her voice was devoid of all emotion.

"You have to think of your girls," he said.

"I know what I'm doing, Harvey. Please, leave us alone."

Harvey turned to me. "Are you bringing charges against Mrs. Lovelace?"

I shook my head. "For the moment, I'm simply gathering information. But, for the record, I have no objection to your staying."

"Go, Harvey," Samantha ordered. "I'll call if I need you."

"But your mother—"

"My mother isn't your client. I am."

"And as my client, you need my advice." The attorney sat in the chair beside her and nodded for me to begin.

Samantha raised her head and looked at me. I had expected tears and drama, but the woman was obviously numb with grief and shock, her eyes red-rimmed and dull.

"You told my mother that Vince was murdered."

I nodded.

She stared out the floor-to-ceiling window at the walled patio garden filled with exotic tropical plants. "Why would anyone want to kill him?"

I should have been the one asking questions, but I let her talk in hopes of gauging her true state of mind. "His death makes you a very rich woman."

"I was already rich. I hated it."

"You hated having money?"

"Things were better before."

"Before?"

"Before Vince struck it rich with his cable network." Light returned to her eyes and the corners of her mouth lifted in an almost smile. "We didn't have money when we were first married, but we had each other."

A tear rolled down her cheek and she brushed it absently with the back of her hand. "But once the network took off, Vince didn't have time for me or the girls. The money was like a drug. The more he made, the more he wanted. I tried everything to get him to spend time with us, but nothing worked."

"Not even Alberto Suarez?"

"You don't have to answer that," Harvey chimed in.

"It's okay, Harvey. I have nothing to hide." Samantha didn't seem surprised that I knew about her affair. "I wanted to make Vince jealous. And I needed someone to pay attention to me. The only thing between Alberto and me was hot sex, and I would have given that up in a heartbeat for one evening at home with my husband."

She took in her breath sharply. "Now I'll never spend an evening with Vince again."

"Did Vince know about you and Alberto?"

"I don't know. He never said anything. I didn't try to hide the affair, but Vince was so busy working, it could have headlined the evening news and he wouldn't have noticed." She lowered her voice until it was almost a whisper. "And I wanted so much for him to notice me."

"Would Alberto have killed Vince out of jealousy?"

"Alberto jealous?" She shook her head. "He's sleeping with half the women at the club."

"What if he thought he could marry you and claim Vince's fortune?"

"Alberto knows I don't love him, that I'd never— Oh, God, I hope he knows that." Her eyes widened with a look of panic. "If he hurt Vince because of me, I couldn't live with the guilt. I have too much shame already."

I could tell she'd been trying to hold herself together ever since I first arrived, but suddenly she lost it, crying in huge, shuddering sobs that racked her entire body. Harvey scrambled for a box of Kleenex.

"I didn't kill my husband, Margaret," she gasped through her tears and mopped her face with the tissues Harvey handed her. "If I'm guilty of anything, it's the stupidity of my affair with Alberto, not murder. I would never do that to my girls. They adore their father." She glared at me through her tears and set her mouth in a hard, thin line. "I'll do everything I can to help catch the bastard who killed my Vince."

"I'll need to talk to your girls. They may know something that will help."

Samantha blew her nose loudly. "Okay, but, please, not today. They're in really bad shape. Jet lag on top of grief. Detective Adler called earlier to say we could return to our house today, and I'm hoping being at home will help them cope. Can you meet us there in the morning?"

"Nine o'clock?" I asked.

She bit her lip as if holding back tears and nodded. "I need to make funeral arrangements, but they won't let me have him. I can't even see his body."

The anguish on her face and in her voice was painful to witness. "I'll check with the medical examiner. Unless she has a problem, the body should be released tomorrow."

Twenty-two years of police work had honed my instincts, and my gut was telling me that Samantha wasn't my killer. Body language, the direction of a person's gaze when she speaks, posture, the tension in her muscles, her respiration rate, and a dozen other tiny gestures and mannerisms that the average person is unaware of tell a trained observer what's going on in a subject's head. Samantha's body was speaking the language of a woman devastated by grief but with nothing to hide.

She continued to sob, and I looked to Harvey. "That's all the questions I have for now."

"I'll take her home," he said.

I returned to my car. Samantha, who'd topped my list of suspects, had now shifted to last place. She, who stood to gain millions, had had the most compelling motive.

But if Samantha hadn't killed her husband, who had?

CHAPTER 10

I parked my car at the Pelican Bay Marina later that afternoon and walked through the sunshine toward Bill's boat. Unseasonably warm weather had daytime temperatures running in the eighties. If I had to partake in a masquerade, I was thankful I could play Mrs. Claus without feeling as if I was at the North Pole.

After leaving the law office, I'd stopped by the station and conferred with Adler, who had been working all morning and had confirmed rock-solid alibis for three of the five people on Elaine Bassett's list of disgruntled employees. The number of suspects in Vince Lovelace's murder was dwindling. With Alberto Suarez looking less like a contender, Dan Rankin, returning from Atlanta tomorrow, and only two unhappy network employees left to interview, prospects of charging someone before Shelton's return were dim. And if I thought today was warm, when the chief got wind of all that had happened while he was gone, tomorrow was going to be a scorcher.

With the box that held my costume tucked under my arm, I approached the *Ten-Ninety-Eight*. In the bright light of late afternoon, the Christmas display of Santa's rattan sleigh pulled by eight prancing flamingos appeared even gaudier than it had in the fog. Bill was waiting at the stern and helped me onto the boat that sat several feet below the dock on the low tide.

"You're not dressed." His disappointment was evident.

"No time," I hedged. "I'll change in the cabin."

Even with his rounded belly, compliments of a plump down pillow, he made an amazingly handsome Saint Nicholas with his thick white hair, sun-burnished face and twinkling blue eyes above a fake thick white mustache and full beard. Fast approaching sixty, Bill had the physique of a much younger man, and in his trim Bermuda shorts and short-sleeved Hawaiian shirt that exposed the tanned, well-developed muscles of his arms and legs, he made a very sexy Santa.

"You're not really into this, are you?" he asked.

I sighed. Bill knew me too well. "I've never been a big fan of Christmas, not even as a kid."

"That's hard to believe. What kid doesn't like Christmas?"

"My mother always hijacked the holiday."

"Your family didn't celebrate?"

"Oh, we celebrated all right, in Mother's own inimitable way. Every room in the house, including the courtyard, was filled with expensive designer trees, delivered by the florist and impeccably trimmed in a special theme. Teams from the florist decorated every windowsill, mantel and banister to match. I felt as if I was living in a department store display window. And I tiptoed around the house on eggshells for the entire holiday, afraid I'd disturb or break something."

I shook my head at the memory. "Caroline loved it, so it must have been me. In addition to missing out on the shopping gene, I didn't inherit the Christmas gene, either."

He pulled me toward him and tipped my chin with his finger until our eyes met. "You don't have to do this—" he nodded toward the box with my costume "—if you don't want to."

I hesitated. Part of me wanted to take the out he'd given me and run. But another part recalled a childhood memory of Daddy, driving me through town and the suburbs to view displays of Christmas lights, with carols playing on the car radio and a stop at the local drive-in for hot chocolate afterward. I longed to reclaim some of that long-lost excitement and sense of wonder. And with Bill so blatantly enthusiastic, I didn't want to rain on his boat parade.

"You've been telling me I need to lighten up and have some fun." I sucked it up and forced a wide smile. "So I'll give it my best shot."

"Good." His responding grin was like an early Christmas present. "But we need to get moving. Why don't you wait until we're under way before changing?"

I started to protest that if I delayed putting on my costume, I might lose my nerve, but he'd already climbed topside to start the engines.

"How about casting off?" he called over his shoulder.

I released the lines and mounted the ladder to the flying bridge. The roar of the powerful engines made conversation impossible, so I settled into a deck chair beside Bill at the controls.

He backed the *Ten-Ninety-Eight* out of its slip and steered toward the channel of the Intracoastal

Waterway to join a queue of other decorated boats sailing south toward the rendezvous point at Island Estates.

I admired the blue-green waters of the sound, the cottonball texture of the mackerel sky and the majestic Washingtonian palms that lined the shore, but my mind wrestled with questions over Vince Lovelace's murder.

Bill cast a glance my way, then leaned over and shouted above the engines. "Don't."

"Don't what?"

"Bring your work along for the ride. You'll miss out on the fun."

His observation shook me. I was forty-eight years old and had spent almost half of my life in police work. When had I forgotten how to relax and enjoy life?

When Greg had been murdered.

But the rationale for my joyless life was harder to recognize. In fact, I'd never really examined my behavior until now. Cruising along the waterway on a boat decked out with tacky flamingos and a ridiculous Mrs. Claus costume waiting for me in the cabin, I had a moment of epiphany.

After Greg had died, I hadn't believed that I deserved to enjoy life. I hadn't known how to live and be happy with Greg dead. Over the years, while memories of Greg had faded and the trauma of his death had lessened, I'd turned my noble suffering into a lifelong habit of working too hard and keeping everyone at arm's length. And twelve years ago, just as I'd begun to lighten up, Daddy's sudden and unexpected death had driven me back into my self-imposed shell.

Enjoy myself, Bill had ordered, but old habits died hard. Having fun was a skill I needed to learn all over again.

I watched Bill at the helm, his eyes shining, fake beard blowing in the wind, a man perfectly at ease as Santa in Jimmy Buffett mode. If I needed an instructor, and I did, to teach me how to lighten up, Bill Malcolm was my guy.

Somehow, in spite of his painful divorce and his daughter's desertion, in spite of years as a cop who had witnessed daily the worst in humanity, he'd hung on to the ability to be happy, to find joy in little moments, to see each day as an adventure. And for most of those years, he'd been my best friend, enduring my joyless outlook on life and prodding me to smile. He'd even asked me to marry him.

God knew, I loved him. But I loved him too

much to impose my gloomy presence on a man who obviously loved life every breathing minute. If I wanted to spend the rest of my days with Bill, I had to learn to be happy again, to regain my sense of playfulness.

No time like the present. I pushed myself from my chair.

"Where are you going?" Bill asked.

"Below." I put my arms around him and placed my lips against his ear. "Santa, baby, you need a wife."

I climbed down toward the cabin to don my costume. I was determined to enjoy myself.

Even if it killed me.

Something magical happened when darkness fell. The convoy of boats, gaudy and pathetic in the harsh light of day, turned into a breathtaking spectacle of fairy lights and fantastic images that floated north in an orderly procession along the channel toward Pelican Bay. Cabin cruisers and sailboats had transformed into gigantic Christmas trees, gaily wrapped boat-size packages, sugarplum fairies, toy soldiers, teddy bears and a plethora of cartoon characters. Sound systems blasted holiday music that carried across the water to the crowds gathered on the shoreline and to those watching from boats anchored along the parade route.

In the tradition of most Christmas parades, the *Ten-Ninety-Eight*, which carried Santa, came last. By the time Bill docked and secured the boat in his usual slip, crowds had moved from the shore to the marina park, where the high school chorus sang "Jingle Bell Rock" in the bandstand and children and their parents gathered to meet Santa.

Bill grabbed a huge red sack trimmed with fake white fur from inside the cabin, hoisted it over his shoulder and stepped onto the dock. He offered me a hand. "Ready, Mrs. Claus?"

I took one look at the people thronging the park and fought the urge to dive back into the cabin. Calling attention to myself had always made me uncomfortable, and as a detective, I'd become adept at blending in and making myself almost invisible. Accompanying Bill, who was definitely the man of the hour, went against the grain. I consoled myself by believing that with my white wig, granny glasses and rouged cheeks, no one would recognize me.

I accepted his hand and fell in step beside him. The kids, waiting in the park, took one look at Bill and went wild. When we reached the end of the dock, the crowd parted, clearing the walkway that led to the bandstand where two gigantic thrones of gilt-painted plywood stood waiting. Bill seated me on his right, then took a seat himself. A line formed instantly of children and parents, all wanting to see Santa.

"What do I do?" I asked in a panic.

Bill took a handful of candy canes from the sack at his feet and gave them to me. "Help me distribute these."

The time passed in a blur of young faces, some excited, others shy or tearful. Only a few stood out, in particular one snotty-nosed little blonde.

"Ain't you got any chocolate?" she demanded. The girl couldn't have been more than eight, with uncombed hair and rumpled clothing. No adult accompanied her.

"Sorry, no chocolate tonight. Where's your mother?" I asked while Bill jostled a three-year-old on his knee and the parents took snapshots.

The girl jerked her thumb over her shoulder toward the Dock of the Bay restaurant. "She's over there, getting a beer. She hates this Christmas crap."

I couldn't turn the child loose in a crowd of strangers, so I tapped Bill on the shoulder. "We're going to find this girl's mother."

He nodded, distracted by another youngster, who was requesting the entire inventory of Toys "R" Us to be delivered by Santa.

With the girl in tow, I crossed the park and entered the Dock of the Bay. I took a few deep breaths to calm my anger at her mother's irresponsibility, sat the girl in a chair in the foyer, and ordered her not to move until I returned with her parent.

"What's your name?" I asked.

"Tiffany," she said.

"What's your last name?"

"Harlow." She glanced around with interest. "My mom said they don't let little kids in here."

Her mother was a liar. Dock of the Bay was a family restaurant. "What's your mother's name?"

"Barbara Harlow."

"I'll be right back."

I skirted the restaurant and went straight to the bar, crowded with patrons. The bartender was adding a paper umbrella to a pink concoction in a hurricane glass.

He glanced up at my approach. "Hi, Maggie. What can I get you tonight?"

So much for my disguise. "I'm looking for a Barbara Harlow. She here?"

He nodded toward a woman at the end of the bar. One word described her. Big. Big hair, big boobs, big butt, big mouth. Her annoying intoxicated laugh, audible above the jukebox, could have peeled the paint off the wall. She was batting her heavily made-up eyes at a burly man beside her and knocking back boilermakers.

I pushed my way through the crowd until I reached her, then tapped her on the shoulder.

"What the hell do you want?" she demanded.

"Your daughter's in the lobby," I said. "You should take her home."

She turned her back on me and took another drink.

I tapped her shoulder again. This time, she swatted my hand away and snarled, "Get lost, Grandma, before I call the cops."

I reached into the pocket of my muumuu, extracted my shield and thrust it in her face. "I am the cops, Ms. Harlow, and if you don't take your daughter home now, I'm arresting you for child abuse."

At the sight of my detective's shield, the woman's burly companion melted into the crowd.

Ms. Harlow was apparently too drunk to think straight. Instead of complying, she leaned toward me with booze-laden breath. "Where's your Christmas spirit, Granny?"

"You've had enough spirits for everyone tonight," I said.

I took her by the elbow and led her toward the front of the restaurant, shouting to the bartender as I passed, "Call us a cab, Bud."

He acknowledged my request with a wave and reached for the phone behind the bar.

In the foyer, Tiffany leaped to her feet, her swagger gone, eyes wide with fright when she spotted her mother. "It's not my fault, Mom. She made me come. I was waiting in the park, just like you said."

The woman raised a hand, as if to slap her daughter, but reined herself in at the last minute. I was almost hoping she'd follow through, just so I could arrest her sorry ass.

"You should never leave Tiffany alone," I said, "especially in a crowded public park at night. The world is full of creeps who wouldn't think twice about carrying her off."

In dismay, I found myself choking up, thinking of the children I'd never had. Between Tiffany and the rugrats visiting Santa, I'd had too many reminders tonight. This woman, who had been blessed with a daughter, had abandoned her. "Don't you know how lucky you are to have her?"

"Lucky?" Barbara said with a sneer. "I can't even have a damn drink without the kid underfoot."

So much for maternal instincts. Harlow had probably evolved from a species that ate their young.

"I've called you a cab," I said. "Go home and sleep it off."

I turned to Tiffany. "And if your mother ever lays a hand on you or leaves you alone again, call 911 and tell them Detective Skerritt said you need someone to come and get you."

"Sure," Tiffany said, but she avoided my eyes when she promised. The girl was obviously afraid of doing anything that would anger her mother.

I left the restaurant after putting the two in a cab. I'd asked the driver to call the station and leave a message for me if Barbara didn't take her daughter straight home. Feeling depressed, I trudged back toward the bandstand, knowing, while I might have saved Tiffany from a mishap tonight, once they had pulled out of sight, she was at the mercy of her mother again.

"Hey, Maggie! Over here."

I turned to see Adler hurrying toward me. He

was wearing jeans and a T-shirt that proclaimed, Observe Wildlife. Be A Cop. His wife Sharon was with him, holding little Jessica in her arms.

"Great boat parade," Adler said. "Malcolm's decorations were spectacular."

"That's one way of putting it," I said.

"We're here to see Santa," Sharon said. "Jessica loves the lights and music."

"Hi, Jessica," I said.

The child smiled and held out her arms. A warm and wonderful feeling slid through me as I took the little girl.

"How do you do that?" Sharon asked. "She's usually really shy around people."

"Must be the Mrs. Claus outfit," I said.

Sharon shook her head. "Has to be you. She did the same thing when you came to her birthday party. She likes you, Maggie."

I hugged Jessica and handed her back to her mother before I embarrassed myself by fogging up my granny glasses. I'd grown fond of this family and, if Adler landed his job with the Clearwater department, they'd soon be moving out of my life, like the other people I'd loved and lost.

"Santa's in the bandstand," I said. "Can Jessica have a candy cane?"

"Sure," Adler said, "if we keep an eye on her with it."

"See you soon." I left them and joined Bill on the platform.

"Is the girl all right?" he asked.

I nodded. "I hope so. I sent her home with her mother."

In a few minutes the Adlers had moved to the front of the line. Bill reached for Jessica, but she retreated into her mother's embrace and wouldn't let Santa hold her. Feeling smug, I gave the little girl a candy cane and was rewarded with a giggle.

"Merry Christmas, sweetie." I couldn't help thinking how my life would have been different if Greg had lived. I'd probably have grandchildren Jessica's age by now. But I hadn't traveled that road and I had no way of backtracking to reclaim what I'd lost.

Seeing all these children had to stir up feelings for Bill, too. His daughter, now married and living on the West Coast, had two children. Bill tried to visit his grandchildren as often as possible, but Melanie had made it clear she didn't want her father in their lives. She was closer to her stepdad. That fact had to hurt him like hell.

The Adlers moved away, and Bill, as if reading my thoughts, grabbed my hand and gave it a squeeze. He leaned toward me and whispered, "You're doing great, Mrs. Claus. When we're through here, how about coming back to my sleigh for a snuggle?"

Before I could reply, Adler reappeared, cell phone in hand. "Just had a call from the station. Another burglary, this one at Al's Attic. Can we take your car?"

"Sorry," I told Bill. "Have to go."

He pulled me toward him and whispered in my ear, "I'll take a rain check on that snuggle."

CHAPTER 11

Al's Attic was a stand-alone building just north of Main Street. A P.B.P.D. cruiser stood in the otherwise empty parking lot when we arrived, and Steve Johnson let us in the front door.

"The alarm company called," Steve said, "to say an alarm had been triggered. No one inside when I arrived, but things are missing."

He was looking at me bug-eyed, but since Johnson often appeared a little squirrelly, I ascribed his expression to the same frustration I was experiencing at another burglary.

I hit several switches in the light panel by the door and fluorescent light flooded the room, a large open area filled with display cases. Glass-fronted shelves lined the walls. Al's Attic wasn't as ordinary as it sounded. The store stocked a variety of high-end collectibles from sports memorabilia and toy action figures to porcelain and crystal figurines, paintings, bronze sculptures and historical artifacts.

Glass from the shelf fronts and display cases littered the aisles, but I had no way of knowing what was missing until the owner did an inventory.

"Forced entry?" I asked Johnson.

He shook his head. "Everything was locked up tight when I arrived. I had to wait for Al to let me in."

"Al's here?" Adler asked.

"Checking her office." Johnson pointed to the rear of the store.

"Al's a her?" I said.

A plump young woman with tangled auburn hair, who had obviously thrown on mismatched clothes in a hurry, came toward us from the office. She stopped a few feet away, cocked her head to one side, looked at me and frowned. "And you are?"

"Detective Maggie Skerritt," I said.

Her puzzled expression remained. "You working undercover?"

Only then did I realize I still wore the white wig, granny glasses and heavy rouge of Mrs. Claus. I must have looked like an escapee from the Golden Years Home for the Aged and Insane. Out of the corner of my eye, I could see Adler biting his lip to keep from laughing, and his shoulders were shaking. I resisted the urge to ram my elbow in his ribs.

"I was taking part in the Christmas celebration at Marina Park." I started to remove the wig, then decided my own hair, plastered to my head all those hours, would make me appear even sillier. I tucked the granny glasses in my pocket, pulled out a tissue and rubbed at my cheeks.

"I appreciate your getting here so quickly," the woman said, but still eyed me as if I was a few beers short of a six-pack. "I'm Alicia Watkins, the owner. I came as soon as the alarm company called. Just checked my office. The door's still locked. Looks like no one's been in there."

"What's missing out here?" I asked.

Adler left the questioning to me and walked toward the rear of the building, searching for a point of entry. The crime scene unit arrived and the techs unpacked their equipment and began their survey.

Alicia did a quick tour of the aisles and examined the broken cases and shelves. "Little stuff, but all very valuable, vintage baseball cards, a Superbowl presentation football, some classic Lladro statuettes, gold coins and—that's odd."

She'd stopped in front of a display of action figures that sat unsecured on top of a counter.

"What's odd?" I asked.

"At least half a dozen of these are missing, but they're only worth a few bucks each. Why would someone steal these?"

Her question confirmed my worst fears. Our thief was most likely a kid who'd decided to take home some souvenirs.

Adler returned. "Came in through the AC system, just like the others. I asked the CSU techs to dust the ductwork."

"We'll need a list with descriptions and values of what's missing," I told Alicia. "But don't touch or disturb anything."

"I'll get on it," she said.

A pounding on the glass at the front door caught my attention. Outside stood a tall, thin, elderly man wearing bedroom slippers and a robe over his pajamas. When he caught my eye, he motioned for me to come out. I hoped he wasn't an Alzheimer's patient, wandering lost and disoriented. I'd have to send Johnson to ID him and take him home. I stepped out the door and closed it behind me.

"You a cop?" He was looking askance at my wig and the shield clipped to my muumuu.

"Detective Maggie Skerritt. What can I do for you?"

He stuck out a bony hand. "Harry Lenkowski, Nassau County, New York, P.D., retired. I live in the condo across the street."

I shook his hand and glanced across the boulevard to the high-rise on the waterfront that overlooked the parking lot of Al's Attic. Bright light streamed from a set of windows on the fifth floor. "What can I do for you?"

He wiped his hand over his thinning hair, then tightened the sash on his robe. "I hope I can do something for you. Looks like you've had a burglary."

"We're still investigating."

"Your perp's a kid on a bike."

"What?"

"I was watching TV, and, being so high up, I leave my windows open for the view. I noticed a kid on a bike circling this place. I didn't think too much about it, except what kind of parents would let their kids ride a bike without lights after dark. Then several minutes later, the outside alarms went off at Al's. I looked out again and saw the kid taking off on his bike like a bat out of hell with a backpack stuffed to the gills. Nobody else in sight. I called 911, but the alarm company had already alerted the police."

"Thanks, Mr. Lenkowski. You've been a big help."

"You need further assistance?" The hunger in his eyes was embarrassing. For an instance, I felt as if I'd been visited by the Ghost of Christmas Future and saw myself retired and alone, longing for the job that had once given my life purpose.

"How about I send Officer Johnson over to your place to take a statement?" I said. "Give him any details you can remember about the kid and the bike."

His face lit up. "That would be great."

"Wait here."

I went inside and told Steve to take the man home and get his statement. Then I filled in Adler on what I'd learned. The fact that I'd been right about someone using kids to do his dirty work gave me no satisfaction. It only increased my determination to catch the slimeball.

"Hey, Detective Skerritt," one of the crime scene techs shouted from a ladder near the open duct. "We've got prints."

"Run 'em as fast as possible." I didn't hold out much hope. Unless the kid had already been through the system, his prints wouldn't be on file.

Fifteen minutes later, Alicia handed me a list of the missing items. I whistled in surprise at their value. "People pay that much for this stuff?"

"It's an investment," she explained. "Hang on to the right collectible and it appreciates faster than blue chip stocks."

I considered the figure again. "But if the stolen items are fenced, they'll bring only ten percent of their worth."

Alicia shook her head. "Not if they sell them through an online auction house. They might make more than they're worth."

Once the techs had finished and Johnson returned from across the street with Lenkowski's statement, we'd done all we could for the evening. The crime unit left, promising to run the prints as soon as possible, and Steve returned to patrol. Alicia Watkins locked her building and drove away.

Adler and I stood on the sidewalk in front of Al's Attic. It was almost midnight.

"I'll go back to the station and file the report," I said.

"It's late. You could wait until morning."

CHARLOTTE DOUGLAS

"Shelton will be back."

"Ah-hh."

He didn't have to say more. We both knew what Shelton's reaction to another murder and burglary would be, and neither of us wanted to witness it firsthand.

I pulled off the wig and ran my fingers through my flattened hair. "I plan to be standing tall at Ted Trask's office first thing tomorrow to find out the particulars of Vincent Lovelace's will. We're running out of leads. Maybe the will shows someone we've missed who stands to profit by Lovelace's death."

"Then you'll see Shelton?"

I shook my head. "After Trask, I'll interview the Lovelace daughters. With any luck, I won't make it back to the station until after lunch." I scratched at the hives on my arms and longed for an oatmeal soak in a tub of hot water.

"I'll be tracking down Rankin first thing tomorrow," Adler said, "and the vic's other disgruntled employees from his secretary's list. Might take me all day."

"If you're lucky. I'll drop you off at home before I file my report."

We climbed into my car.

"Maggie?"

"Yeah?"

"What you did tonight was outstanding."

"This was just a routine call."

He shook his head. "I'm talking about you and Bill playing Santa for the kids."

"You can thank Malcolm for that. I was merely a reluctant accomplice."

"Yeah, right." Adler was grinning as if he knew a secret.

"What?"

"You're a natural with kids."

I didn't know what to say, so I kept my mouth shut. But as I drove through the quiet streets, it wasn't the children whose parents had brought them to see Santa who were on my mind. I was worrying about Tiffany Harlow and the children who'd been trained as rooftop burglars.

The offices of Trask, Farmingham and Lane were in the SunTrust building on the corner of Main Street, a block from the marina. I'd last visited Ted Trask there a month ago while investigating the weight-loss clinic murders. The second victim had lived next door to Trask on exclusive Pelican Point.

While the elevator carried me to the law offices two floors above the bank, I scratched the back of my right leg with the toe of my left foot. Not even an early-morning oatmeal bath had alleviated the torment of my hives. If Trask didn't give me a significant lead, I'd have to schedule an appointment with a dermatologist.

The door slid open on the luxurious suite. I went straight to Trask's secretary, who frowned when I asked to see him.

"Do you have an appointment?" the Mrs. Doubtfire look-alike asked.

"Only this." I showed her my shield.

"Might work," she said.

"Hate to have to get a warrant." It was an empty threat, but effective.

She reached hastily for the intercom and announced my presence. The door to Trask's office flew open and a tall, trim man in an Italian suit motioned me inside.

"I thought I'd be seeing you when I heard about Vince," Trask said. "What a tragedy. Eudora, bring us coffee, please, and Vincent Lovelace's file."

He closed the door. "Have a seat, Detective."

Trask sat behind his desk, a slab of black marble on stainless-steel columns. Behind him, visible through the floor-to-ceiling glass windows, stretched a panoramic view of the bayfront with the water sparkling in the early morning light.

"You're handling Lovelace's estate?" I asked.

Trask leaned back in his chair, formed a steeple with his fingers and peered at me over the tips. "Not much to handle, at this point."

"I heard he was worth at least a billion."

The attorney shook his head. "I meant, his estate's not complicated. Everything's in a trust, which became irrevocable upon his death."

Eudora bustled in, coffee tray in her hands, a file tucked under her arm. She placed the tray on a side table and gave Trask the folder, then handed me a cup of coffee, complete with the cream and sugar I'd requested, and served her boss.

"Anything else, Mr. Trask?" she asked.

"That will be all, Eudora. Thank you." He shook his head once she'd closed the door behind her. "Don't know what I'll do when she retires next month."

I took a sip of the coffee that was almost as good as Dunkin' Donuts'. "Who are the recipients of Lovelace's trust?"

"Only one. Everything goes to Samantha, then to the girls upon their mother's death."

"That's it? No other bequests or parting gifts?" That wasn't what I wanted to hear, since it left me at a dead end. The tip of my nose was aflame and I resisted the urge to scratch.

Trask flipped through the pages from the file, scanned each sheet and shook his head. "Vince Lovelace was only thirty-eight and in the peak of health. He obviously wasn't expecting to die so soon."

"Comes as a surprise to most of us." I set my cup aside and stood. "Thanks for your help."

My beeper sounded as I was riding down in the elevator. I stopped in the bank lobby, asked to use a courtesy phone and dialed Adler's cell.

"Rankin's clean," he said. "Had fifteen guests Thanksgiving Day who can vouch that he never left his house and his boat never left its slip."

"No luck at the attorney's, either. Vince left everything to his wife, so no other leads with a motive. Any luck with the employees?"

"I'm on them now. According to Rankin, they both took jobs at another network and moved out of state. Neither of them had the guts, in his words, to hurt anybody. So where does that leave us?"

"Up the proverbial creek. I'm on my way to the

beach. I'll meet you back at the station after lunch."

"You think Shelton will have chilled by then?"

"Has hell frozen over?"

"Good point. And good luck."

CHAPTER 12

But my luck wasn't good. Isabelle met me at the door of the Lovelace home with blood in her eye.

"You should be ashamed, Margaret Skerritt, tormenting this poor family after all that's happened."

"I'm just doing my job. If it wasn't me, it would be someone else. Your son-in-law was murdered. Don't you want his killer found?"

"You're not accusing my Samantha?"

"Everyone's a suspect until the killer is identified. And until we find out who killed Vince and why, Samantha and the girls might be in danger. I don't want to see them hurt, do you?"

"Are you trying to frighten me?"

I shook my head. "Someone had reason to knock Vince into the pool and hold him under until he drowned. At this point, we don't know who or why. It may be a long shot, but it is conceivable that whoever killed Vince might also want to harm Samantha and your granddaughters. But I won't know for sure until the killer's caught. And I can't catch the murderer without the cooperation of Samantha and her girls."

Isabelle pressed her lips together as if biting back words and ushered me into the living room. The Lovelace daughters sat on either side of their mother on the sofa. In spite of my intentions to remain objective, I felt a rush of pity. Without the usual makeup and veneer of sophistication most girls their age affected, they looked like lost children. Their eyes were swollen from crying, and each clasped one of her mother's hands. The scene was a vignette of sadness in the midst of the room's bright and cheerful colors.

"Margaret," Samantha said with a nod of acknowledgment. "Can we get this over with quickly?"

"Emily, Dana," I said, "I'm sorry for your loss, and I'm sorry to bother you at a time like this with questions. But my job is to find who killed your father, and I need your help."

"How can we help?" Emily, the older teen, asked. "We weren't even here."

"I know. Your mother's explained that. But I want you to think back to the days and weeks before Thanksgiving. Did you notice anyone suspicious in the neighborhood? Strangers you hadn't seen before?"

"Nobody gets on the street past the gate." Dana wiped her nose with the back of her hand. "But there's always strangers on the beach. Even though the property's posted, they stroll by all the time."

"Did any of them seem particularly interested in this house?"

Samantha heaved an exasperated sigh. "Of course they did, Margaret. It's an architectural masterpiece. People are always gawking at the place."

"Wait," Emily said. "There was one guy."

"On the beach?" I asked.

She shook her head. "In a boat. He was anchored off the beach the past few weekends."

Samantha shook her head. "Still nothing unusual about that. Fishermen do it all the time."

"Yeah, but this guy wasn't fishing," Dana said. "I remember him, too. Gave me the creeps, 'cause he was studying the house through binoculars. I saw him from my bedroom window a couple times."

"Why didn't you tell me?" Samantha asked.

Dana shrugged and avoided her mother's gaze.

"You've been…distracted lately. And Dad was never home."

"Tell me about this man and his boat," I said. "What do you remember?"

"He stayed offshore," Emily said, "so I couldn't get a good look at him."

"Young? Old? Tall? Fat? Help me out, girls."

"He was tall," Dana said, "and he looked young, at least from a distance."

"What color hair?"

"He wore a ball cap," Emily said. "And sunglasses."

"And you're sure he was watching the house?"

Dana nodded. "But when Dad would come out for his swim, the guy would weigh anchor and leave."

"I thought you said your dad was never home."

"The guy always showed up in the late afternoon," Emily explained, "right before Dad had his swim."

"So why didn't you tell your father about him?" Samantha demanded.

"Because after his swim, Dad always went to his office and didn't want to be disturbed."

"Describe the boat," I said.

"A cigarette boat," Dana replied.

Bingo. "Did you see the registration number?"

The girls shook their heads. "It was too far out," Emily said, "but I read the name on the stern."

"Me, too," Dana said. "It was *Jackpot*."

I looked to Samantha. "Know anyone with a cigarette boat named *Jackpot*?"

She shook her head. "Our family's never been into boating."

Just tennis, I thought, but for the sake of her daughters, held my tongue.

Determined to postpone facing Shelton's hissy fit, I stopped by the Pelican Bay Marina instead of returning to the station. Bill was dismantling the *Ten-Ninety-Eight*'s Christmas display. Portable drill in hand, he greeted me with a wave and a smile. Having someone glad to see me was a pleasant change.

I pointed to the flamingos stacked on the dock. "What will you do with them?"

"Fernandez says I can store them in his garage for next year."

Now there was a happy thought. Next year I'd get to play Mrs. Claus all over again. "Sorry I had to take off last night."

"Another burglary?"

I nodded. "A witness saw a kid on a bike flee-ing the scene."

"Did the kid have a name?"

"No, but he left prints. If he's in the system, I'll have him by this afternoon."

Bill added another pink plywood carcass to the stack. "Can you stay for lunch?"

"Why are you always trying to feed me?"

He grinned. "It works on stray dogs."

"What?"

"Feed 'em and they keep coming back."

"You're saying I remind you of a stray dog?"

"I'm saying I want you always to come back." He landed a kiss on my mouth as he stepped past to board.

"Like a boomerang." His words shook me more than I cared to admit.

"Or a rubber ball. You'll come bouncing back to me."

"Now you're showing your age. That line's from an old Simon and Garfunkel tune, isn't it?"

He opened the sliders to the cabin. "The good old days."

I followed him inside. "This conversation is making me feel ancient."

"You know what they say." He moved into the

galley and I sat on the love seat in the lounge. "Inside every older lady is a much younger woman."

"Yeah, and the one in me is screaming, 'What the hell happened?'"

"You were terrific last night, Margaret."

"I'd take that as a compliment, but I wasn't here last night."

"At the boat parade and in the park. You made a great Mrs. Claus."

I propped my feet on the coffee table and clawed the hives on the back of my hands. "Guess I'm destined for mature roles from here on out."

"Cut it out!" The sharpness in his voice surprised me. "You're only forty-eight. You're in great shape and you look fantastic."

Compliments made me uncomfortable. "I hope you can say the same after Shelton's through with me today."

"Maybe the chief will be reasonable for a change."

"Reasonable? Don't you know the old adage that claims if a kid wets the bed and tortures animals, he'll grow up to be either a serial killer or chief of police?"

"Or to work in Internal Affairs," Bill added with a straight face. He had assembled the ingredients for sandwiches on the counter and began construction. "Any luck on the Lovelace case?"

"As a matter of fact, I might have my first real lead." I explained what the girls had told me about the cigarette boat. "Now all I have to do is find the damn thing."

"Let me."

"Why would you want to?"

"To save your skin." He pointed to the backs of my hands, inflamed from hives and scratching. "Besides, I like hanging around boats and marinas. This would give me an excuse."

"What if this cigarette boat is docked at one of thousands of private slips in the bay area?"

"Cigarette boats are a specialty. Not too many mechanics work on them. If it's not moored in a public marina, I can track it down through dealers, mechanics or paint distributors."

He placed the top slice of bread on each sandwich, cut them into halves with a chef's knife and passed one to me. "If you plan to go several rounds with the chief this afternoon, you'll need your strength. Eat up."

I stared at the six-inch-high monster he'd concocted.

"Something wrong?" he asked.

"The sandwich is fine. I was just thinking about Shelton."

"And?"

"Things are going to get a lot worse before they get worse."

With a sense of fatalism, I took a bite.

I got out of my car at the station and noted that Shelton's parking space was empty. Restraining myself from a happy dance, I hurried into the building to meet Adler, hoping we could compare notes before Shelton returned from his lunch break.

Adler was at his desk, polishing off a large pizza with onions, pepperoni and anchovies. The kid was always eating and never gained a pound, further proof that life was not fair.

"There's one slice left, Maggie. You want it?"

"I already ate. Don't you ever get indigestion?"

"Nope." He bit into the last slice.

"Then you have something to look forward to when you get older."

"Bad morning?"

"Good, actually." I told him about *Jackpot* and Bill's offer to track the boat.

He wiped tomato sauce from his hands with a

paper napkin. "Maybe the new lead will keep Shelton off our backs."

"And maybe the Devil Rays will win the series. What did you find out?"

"We can scratch Rankin and the last two employees from our list. All had alibis."

"So our mystery man on the cigarette boat is our only viable lead."

"Lovelace's girls didn't know him?"

I shook my head. "But that doesn't mean Vince didn't. Bill says he'll start his search at the yacht club, then expand from there."

I stared at the grid of suspects on my desk. All had been eliminated except the question mark at the bottom of the list. "If he's our guy, he apparently cased the house for weeks before moving in for the kill."

"Maybe he's a sicko who looks for opportunity, then murders for the thrill."

"If that's the case, then we can expect another murder. Soon."

"Skerritt!" Shelton's voice bellowed down the hall. "Get in here."

"Can't let you have all the fun," Adler said. "Want me to come, too?"

I shook my head. "Call the CSU lab. See if they've had a hit on those prints from last night."

Adler nodded. "Anything else?"

"If I'm not back in thirty minutes, call the mortuary."

Shelton sat at his desk and blew his nose into a handful of Kleenex. His eyes were red and bloodshot, his nose bulbous and shining. For a man who'd just returned from vacation, he looked as if he'd come off a three-day drunk.

"Have a good holiday?" I asked.

He scowled at me with bleary eyes. "Myra was sick with the flu the whole damn time."

Myra, his bleached-blond trophy wife, while curvaceous and attractive in a blatantly sexual way, had an IQ slightly above that of an amoeba.

"Sorry to hear that. I hope she's feeling better."

"I was stuck in a cabin in the wilderness for five whole days. Couldn't go anywhere because I had to take care of her."

"At least you got some rest."

"Rest? There was only one TV, which, unfortunately, got some friggin' soap opera channel that she watched incessantly. It was worse than water torture." He tossed one wad of tissues into the wastebasket and grabbed another. "And if that wasn't bad enough, this place has gone to hell in a handbasket while I've been gone."

Shelton was on a rant, and I knew better than to interfere. I might as well try to stop a volcano from erupting.

"A murder, for chrissakes, and another robbery! All in less than a week. Doesn't anyone do his job around here?"

"We have prints from the latest robbery. We're waiting for an ID."

He slapped the surface of his desk with the palm of his hand. "Not good enough! I want a suspect in the Lovelace murder behind bars. The press is all over this like ugly on a toad. You know the vulnerable position the department's in."

"We also have a lead in the Lovelace case."

"Is an arrest imminent?"

I mentally calculated how long Bill might take to locate *Jackpot*. "Possibly within the week."

"I want an arrest today."

"I can't pull a suspect out of thin air."

"You won't have to." He picked up the folder that held the initial reports from the case. "You have a suspect with means, motive and opportunity. I want Samantha Lovelace arrested today, in time to make the six-o'clock news."

I'd been standing till that moment, but I sank into the chair in front of his desk. "But Samantha didn't do it."

He tried to pierce me with a stare, but his rheumy eyes spoiled the effect. "And you know this how?"

"I've interviewed her."

"That's it?" His voice was heavy with congestion and sarcasm. "She *told* you she didn't do it?"

"Give me some credit, Chief. I've questioned hundreds of suspects in my career. Samantha Lovelace wasn't lying."

"I understand she's a friend of yours."

I shook my head. "Her mother and mine are best friends."

His grin was brutal. "So we have a little problem called conflict of interest."

My position looked bad and nothing I could say would improve it, so I kept quiet.

"If we don't make an arrest," he said, "we're giving our political opponents fodder for their cause. I don't know about you, Skerritt, but I want to keep my job."

I shook my head. "It's not going to happen."

"It damned well better happen. I've given you an order."

"I'm talking about keeping the department. Ulrich paid me a visit while you were gone."

"The councilman?"

"He wanted to enlist my public endorsement of his plan to bring in the sheriff's department. Offered me a promotion in the sheriff's CID if I'd cooperate."

Shelton was gathering steam for another blowup, so I added quickly, "I turned him down. But how well our department performs is a moot point in this debate. It's all politics and the fix is in. Ulrich has aspirations to higher office, and pushing this county one step closer to a metro government will earn him political capital with the big boys."

Shelton reeled back in his chair as if I'd slapped him. "You're sure?"

"I know you don't like me, Chief, but have I ever lied to you?"

His reddened face turned ashen. "If we keep on our toes, the people will support us. Even Ulrich and his political machine can't fake a vote."

I almost felt sorry for him. "You're grasping at straws. The turnout in a city election is minimal.

All Ulrich has to do is mobilize the party volunteers to turn additional voters out. A few hundred extra votes are all they'll need to turn the tide in their favor. Everything legal and above board. And we're history."

Shelton sat very still as the implications sank in.

"So," I said gently, hoping to drive home the point, "arresting Samantha Lovelace isn't necessary."

The chief said nothing and I began to relax, thinking that he'd seen the reason in what I'd told him. I rose from my chair and started for the door.

"Skerritt." His voice whipped across the room with its old authority. "From what you've told me, good PR is our only hope. Arrest the wife."

"But, Chief—"

"If you don't, I will."

I could picture the scene, Shelton and an entourage of reporters and cameraman descending on the Lovelace house, and Samantha in handcuffs splattered across the evening news and tomorrow's headlines.

"I'll do it," I said.

"Do it now."

At my desk, I put in a call to Harvey Dykeman. "I have bad news," I said when he came on the line.

"I'm listening."

"The chief wants Samantha arrested."

"On what charge?"

"Murder one. I'm giving you a heads-up." I kept my voice low. Shelton would have my hide if he'd known what I was doing.

"You want me to be at the house when you come for her?" the attorney asked.

"No, I want you to bring her in. Very quietly, under the radar. I'll arrange for an officer to sneak you in through the sally port. Shelton wants publicity. I can't keep the arrest out of the papers, but I can give her some privacy. If you bring her in at three, you can push for an early arraignment, maybe get her released on her own recognizance so she doesn't have to spend a night in jail. And if she's released before the media get wind of the arrest, there'll be no photographers, no embarrassing video."

"Thanks, Detective. I have some friends who are judges. Maybe I can pull a few strings of my own. We'll be at the station at three."

Adler, whose desk was practically on top of mine, had heard every word. "You're sticking your neck out."

"So Shelton fires me. The way I see it, we'll all

be out of a job after the February referendum anyway. Besides, Samantha didn't kill her husband. She doesn't need this extra grief."

The phone rang and Adler grabbed it. He scribbled on the pad on his desk, thanked the caller and hung up. "We got a hit on the prints from Al's Attic."

"Anyone we know?"

"Oh, yeah. Jason McLeod."

"Why am I not surprised?"

Twelve-year-old Jason was the boy who'd stumbled over Peter Castleberry's body on the Pinellas Trail several weeks ago. The boy had a rap sheet going back four years, and why he'd never been sent to juvenile detention was one of life's mysteries. He lived with his alcoholic single mother who earned her booze money and their meager living on her back, leaving Jason essentially to fend for himself. But the kid had a sweet, angelic appearance, and whenever he'd appeared in court, his mother would accompany him and cry. Up until now, soft-hearted judges had always released him to her custody. And he kept showing up like a bad penny after committing petty crimes all over town. His innocent demeanor and weeping mom wouldn't wiggle him out of this one.

"Call the middle school," I said. "Ask the vice principal to detain him until we get there."

Adler dialed the school and spoke to the secretary. While he was on hold, I considered how to convince Jason to turn on his mentor, a predator who enlisted kids to steal for him. After a life spent primarily on the streets, Jason wasn't afraid of anything, certainly not the police. He showed unwavering allegiance to the criminal code. And he wouldn't snitch.

Adler spoke to the vice principal, then hung up the receiver. "The kid skipped school today."

"Poor baby. He had a late night. He's probably sleeping in."

"Want me to pick him up at home?"

I checked my watch. "Dykeman will be bringing Samantha in soon. I want you to go with me to transport her to the county jail. The sooner she's there, the quicker she's arraigned and hopefully released. We can collar Jason on the way back."

Adler nodded, then took a flyer off his desk and handed it to me. "The department Christmas party is at our house next weekend."

"Under the circumstances, you think anyone will feel like partying?"

He shrugged. "It might be the last Christmas together for us as a department. I'm hoping it'll be special."

"More like a wake."

"Where's your Christmas spirit?"

"Just call me Ebenezer."

"The party's potluck."

"You know I don't cook."

"So get takeout. Better yet, bring Malcolm and let him cook. If we're lucky, he'll make his famous bread pudding I've heard about."

I couldn't help smiling. Bill had found this outrageous recipe for a bread pudding on the Food Network. It started with a dozen Krispy Kreme glazed donuts. To the crumbled pastries, he added raisins, a custard mixture of eggs and cream, and a generous cup of Jack Daniel's. Amazingly, that concoction baked up into one of the most sinfully delectable desserts I'd ever tasted. And, because it was made with donuts, Bill alternately dubbed it Police Pudding or Cop Custard, depending on his mood. It was a major artery-clogger, but also a crowd-pleaser.

"I'll ask him," I said. "He likes parties."

"And you don't?"

"About as much as a pig does a barbecue."

Adler grinned. "Guess that qualifies you as a party animal."

"Yeah, if I get too wild, I'll count on you to hold me back." I checked the clock. "Let's head for the sally port. Dykeman will be arriving soon, and I want us to handle this. If we're lucky, we'll get Samantha in and out before anyone else sees her."

Two hours later we were stuck in going-home traffic on the Bayside Bridge, edging north on McMullen-Booth Road. Between our efforts at stealth and the strings Dykeman had pulled, Samantha had been booked, arraigned and released in record time. In the back seat of Dykeman's Lexus with tinted windows, she had been driven away from the county judicial complex before the media had gotten wind of the arrest. The charges would still make the six-o'clock news and the morning headlines, but by then, Samantha would be sequestered in the privacy of her home.

We were headed back to Pelican Bay to pick up Jason McLeod. A hundred feet in front of us the road narrowed to two lanes where bulldozers and dump trucks worked on an overpass.

"Ever wonder," Adler said, "why the DOT waits until the height of tourist season to begin road projects? Every north-south artery in the county is under construction."

"Murphy's Law?" I said, but my thoughts were on Jason McLeod. I'd witnessed his four-year slide into a life of crime, but I'd been powerless to stop it. I felt the same frustration over the plight of Tiffany Harlow, who remained at the mercy of her negligent mother. The state's Department of Children and Families did their best, but, like most large and unwieldy government agencies, DCF often operated with the same twisted logic and inefficiency as DOT. What these kids needed was immediate intervention and mentors who could keep them on the right track. Such help might come too late for Jason, but there were dozens like him in Pelican Bay who might profit from a nudge in the right direction. In the back of my mind, a plan was formulating, but I'd need help to implement it.

"We're moving," Adler said. "Maybe we'll get to McLeod's before dark after all."

CHAPTER 13

Adler had been too optimistic. Between road construction and a lane-blocking traffic accident, we took another hour to reach Pelican Bay. Adler turned east into a subdivision of homes built in the sixties in what had once been an orange grove. Aging citrus trees, sickly survivors, dotted the front yards of many of the austere houses built from concrete blocks. Unlike the more affluent neighborhoods where lush green lawns and tropical landscaping were the norm, barren stretches of gray, sandy soil and patches of sandspurs and weeds surrounded these houses.

Tourists like to think of Florida as a verdant paradise. The truth is, without tons of fertilizer, gallons of reclaimed water and hours of constant vigilance against pests and diseases, little grows in most parts of the state except saw palmettos, scrub oaks and pines. The residents of this neighborhood obviously had neither the time nor money to spend on horticulture.

The McLeod house was even more derelict than its sad neighbors. Paint faded and peeled from its cinder-block walls, torn screens hung from the windows and a thick coat of mildew blackened what had once been a white tile roof. Adler turned into the driveway and parked behind a rusting blue Chevy Cavalier in the carport. In the gathering twilight, the dark house exuded an atmosphere of unhappiness and neglect.

"Sheesh," Adler muttered. "No wonder the kid never stays home."

"Let's hope he's home now." I opened the car door, climbed out, picked my way along the broken sidewalk and tried not to stumble in the dark.

I pushed the doorbell and heard no corresponding ring through the open jalousie windows, so I pounded on the door. Inside, someone grunted in surprise, as if awakened from sleep, and made fumbling sounds in the darkness. In seconds, a light shone through the front windows, footsteps approached and the low-wattage bare bulb above the front porch clicked on with a sickly yellow glare.

"Who is it?" a gravelly voice asked.

"Mrs. McLeod?"

"Yeah?" she answered hesitantly.

"It's Detective Skerritt with the Pelican Bay Police."

The jalousie door swung inward and, jaundiced by the porch light, a young woman with ratted hair, bleary eyes, and wearing faded shorts and a T-shirt, glared at me. The smell of booze oozed from her pores. "What's the little shit done now?"

"Is Jason home?" I asked.

She turned toward the inside of the house and bellowed, "Jason, get your butt out here!"

Adler, I noted, had slipped from the car and headed around back, in case Jason decided to make a run for it out a rear door.

No sound emanated from the darkened remainder of the house.

"Guess he ain't here," Mrs. McLeod said.

"Do you mind if I check?"

"Is his bike in the carport?"

"I didn't see it."

"Then he's out with his buddies."

"Do you know where?"

She shrugged. "Wherever it is boys go. You're welcome to look around if you like, but he ain't here."

I walked through the tiny living room with its

L-shaped dining area, glanced into the kitchen, its counters piled high with dirty dishes, then entered a hallway. Soiled clothes and clutter littered the furniture and floors, and just walking through the house was like crossing a minefield. The place should have had a warning sign: Do Not Enter Without Proper Vaccinations!

Jason was nowhere to be found, but in the disaster area Mrs. McLeod identified as his room, I discovered in plain sight a group of action figures, new and in the box, with Al's Attic price stickers on them. By now, Adler had joined me and I had him bag the toys and take them to the car.

"Your son's in a lot of trouble, Mrs. McLeod," I told her. "For his sake, you'd better tell me where he is before he gets hurt."

"He hangs out on the Trail with his pals. That's the only place I know to look when I can't find him." She reached to her throat and fingered a gold dolphin with a diamond eye attached to a heavy gold chain. The necklace matched the description of one stolen from Bloomberg's jewelry store.

I pointed to her throat. "I'll have to take your necklace."

Her fist tightened around the bauble. "Jason gave it to me for my birthday."

"It was stolen from Bloomberg's during a break-in last week."

She shook her head stubbornly. "It's mine. I ain't never had anything so purty."

I took a deep breath. "Look, Mrs. McLeod, you either hand over the necklace or I arrest you for receiving stolen property and take you in. It's your call."

She took a moment to consider her options, then unclasped the chain and handed the jewelry to me. "I don't know why you cops keep picking on me and my boy."

Obviously the poor woman didn't have a clue. And having been raised by an idiot, Jason hadn't had a chance.

"If Jason comes home before we find him, you'll be doing him a favor if you bring him in yourself."

She shook her head and laughed. "What? Do you think I'm stupid?"

Some questions required no answers. I let myself out the front door and joined Adler in the car.

Fifteen minutes later we were parked at the intersection of the Trail and Windward Lane. The Pinellas Trail, a former railroad bed turned into a thirty-eight-mile-long linear park, was a favorite haunt of joggers, cyclists, pedestrians and criminals who wanted a quick and unobserved getaway. Adler killed the lights.

"Do we wait for them to come to us," he asked, "or go find the little buggers?"

"Let's search," I said. "We need to grab Jason before his mother tips him off that we're on to him and he disappears into the woodwork."

Adler removed an eighteen-inch Maglite from beneath the seat. I took a much smaller version from the pocket of my blazer and climbed out of the car. Adler was watching me and grinning.

"What?"

"Ever notice," he said, "how the longer you've been a cop, the shorter your flashlight gets?"

"And your temper," I warned him. "Let's head north, but don't turn your light on yet. There's enough moonlight to make our way. And we don't want to spook Jason."

Adler shook his head. "That's one cold-blooded kid. I doubt an atomic blast would spook him."

In silence, we walked toward town. The Trail was unlighted and officially closed at sunset. Unofficially, everyone from dog walkers to cat burglars used it whenever they pleased. Tonight, however, the asphalt path was deserted with the only sounds the noise of televisions drifting from the houses that backed up to the Trail, the occasional hum of traffic on a nearby street and the eerie call of a screech owl.

Halfway between Windward and the next inter-secting street, Adler stopped, placed his hand on my arm and jerked his head to the right. From the cover of a thick stand of Brazilian pepper bushes came muted hip-hop music. At least, I assumed that's what it was. Sounded like a herd of elephants dancing on pots and pans.

Closer inspection of the bushes revealed a dim light glowing in the middle of them. The wind shifted and the night reeked with the stench of pot.

I nodded to Adler and motioned to the left. He circled the bushes on that side and I moved around on the right. When Adler was in position, I aimed my flashlight into the center of the bushes and turned it on.

"Police," I called. "Come out with your hands up."

The bushes exploded as two boys leaped to their feet to try to escape, but Adler blinded them with his Maglite.

"Hands in the air, Jason," I ordered again. "And your friend, too. What's your name, son?"

"Up yours!"

"Okay, Up Yours, you have the right to remain silent…."

An hour later, alone in a holding cell at the station, Up Yours was more cooperative. He told us his name was Richard Denny, and he gave us his parents' address and phone number.

Denny was our second burglar, all right. I could tell instantly, once I got a good look at him in the station's bright lights. Tall and scrawny, he was wearing the same clothes he'd worn in the surveillance video taken of the burglary at Bloomberg's.

But, as I'd feared, neither Jason nor Denny would give up whoever had recruited them for the robberies. I figured their ringleader was one mean dude, since they both were more terrified of him than of going to jail. My only consolation was that Jason and Richard, charged with grand theft and drug possession and locked up in juvenile detention, would be committing no more crimes. Now all I had to do was to catch the mastermind behind their burglaries before he trained new recruits. With the boys refusing to squeal, my best hope was Mick Rafferty and his facial recognition software, and Mick had promised me results soon.

"Have Johnson and Beaton transport our guests to the juvenile lockup," I told Adler. "Then go home and spend some time with your family."

"What about you?"

"I'll write up the report on our young felons and leave it on Shelton's desk so he'll have it first thing tomorrow."

Adler leaned against the door frame, his arms crossed over his chest, and looked at me.

"What?" I asked.

"You know, Maggie, I'm really going to miss you."

"Get outta here, before I put you back to work."

He grinned, waved and left.

I grabbed a tissue, blew my nose and pulled up an arrest report form on my computer.

The Monday night football game blared from the television above the crowded bar when I met Bill an hour later at the Dock of the Bay. A quick scan of the patrons' faces confirmed Barbara Harlow's absence, but I had no way of knowing whether she'd abandoned Tiffany tonight for some other watering hole.

Instead of sitting across the booth from me,

225

Bill slid in beside me after I sat down. I scooted over to make room and threw him a questioning look.

"I'm still waiting for my rain check on that snuggle," he said with a suggestive wiggle of his eyebrows. "Plus the noise level's so high, I don't think you can hear me unless I talk into your ear."

He had a practical point, but I also found myself enjoying the comfort of his thigh pressed against mine and his arm, laid along the headrest behind me, in an almost embrace. Being with Bill was like being wrapped in a favorite old quilt, warm and comforting. And, after Shelton's earlier tirade, I needed warmth and comfort.

We placed our orders, the waitress brought our drinks, and I gave Bill the rundown on Shelton's hissy fit, Samantha's subsequent booking and the arrests of Jason McLeod and Richard Denny.

"You've had quite a day," he said when I'd finished.

I scratched my forearms. "I need a break in this murder case. Between my hives, Shelton and my mother, it's driving me nuts. Any luck on the cigarette boat?"

"I know where it's not." He paused while the waitress served our plates. "I've checked every marina in Pelican Bay, Dunedin and Clearwater. No sign of any boat named *Jackpot*."

I poured a dollop of ketchup on my plate and dabbed a French fry in it. "Those marinas are closest to the Lovelace place. Maybe our killer stays far away from home."

"Doesn't like to foul his own nest?"

I nodded. "But you've only hit a fraction of the marinas in the Tampa Bay area. Your search could take weeks. If he's killing at random, I'm worried he'll strike again."

"I've been on the phone to mechanics and boat painters. So far, none of them know a boat named *Jackpot*. But I have a lead that could be helpful. Name of a mechanic at a marina at Rocky Point off the Tampa causeway. He works on nothing but cigarette boats. He'll be my first call tomorrow."

He said nothing for a moment. The usual twinkle in his eyes was missing, replaced by an uncommon sadness.

"You okay?" I asked.

"Yeah." But his corresponding sigh contradicted his words. "While I was in Tampa today, I visited my dad."

Bill checked in on his father in the Alzheimer's wing of the assisted-living facility at least twice a week. Some visits turned out better than others. From the look on his face, today's had been rough.

"How is he?" I asked.

Bill shrugged. "He seems content. He's getting good care."

"But?"

"He didn't recognize me at all today. Not even when I explained who I am. He can't even remember that he has a son." Bill's usually cheerful expression twisted with pain. "He's still alive, but he's gone. And it hurts like hell."

I covered his hand with mine. "I'm sorry. If he doesn't know you're there, maybe it would be easier on you if you didn't go."

"I have to visit, because I'd know if I wasn't there, even if Dad didn't." He squeezed my fingers hard, cleared his throat and changed the subject. "Like, I said, I'll check out the boat mechanic tomorrow."

"You sure you want to do this?" I worried that I was taking advantage of his friendship and good nature. "Wouldn't you rather be boating, as your car bumper sticker says?"

"Hell, Maggie, I'm having fun tracking this boat. I hadn't realized how much I missed the job until I started helping you with your cases."

I shook my head. "We're a pair, aren't we? You urging me to have more fun, while you're busting your butt to do more work."

"Balance." He dropped his arm around my shoulders for a hug. "That's the key."

"It's hard to find balance with my job. I'm either working 24/7 on a case or sitting at the station and twiddling my thumbs."

"It wouldn't be that way if we were our own bosses."

"You are your own boss."

"I'm talking about a private investigation firm. You've said the department's finished after the February referendum. If we set up our own P.I. business, we can call the shots."

"Such as no divorce cases? I refuse to tail errant spouses to photograph them in compromising situations. I'd be terminally depressed."

"No divorce cases, if that's what you want."

He'd mentioned the possibility of our own P.I. firm before, but for the first time, I was beginning to take him seriously. "You think we'd have any other business with that exclusion?"

He chewed a mouthful of burger and swallowed. "Missing persons, background checks for businesses, maybe even an occasional security detail.

That would be enough. We have to leave time for fun."

"I keep forgetting fun."

"I know." His expression turned serious. "And I can't let you do that."

"I'm an old dog, Malcolm, and unlikely to learn new tricks."

His expression darkened and his eyes turned sad. "You'll have to, Margaret, for our sakes."

He looked so serious, I felt a shiver of apprehension. "For our sakes?"

He nodded and pushed away his half-eaten burger. "I retired early so I can enjoy life. I don't want to go back to the same rut I was in for almost thirty years."

"Then why become a P.I.?"

"Because I don't mind working some. And the extra money will allow us to enjoy things we couldn't otherwise afford."

"Then why so solemn?"

"The operative words are *fun* and *enjoy*. You have a terrific sense of humor, Margaret, and somewhere under that tough workaholic exterior is a wonderful woman yearning to take pleasure from all the opportunities life has to offer. You've just forgotten how, and you need to relearn."

I struggled to breathe. "I hear an 'or else' in there somewhere."

He didn't shake his head or deny it. "I'm almost sixty. A man my age might live another thirty years—or I could check out tomorrow. I don't have time to waste. I want to live what days or years I have left to the fullest."

"But not with a stick-in-the-mud like me?" I was in shock, unable to contemplate a life without him in it.

"You haven't heard what I'm saying. You're not a stick-in-the-mud at heart. You just have to learn to let go. To lighten up."

A fist closed around my heart. "What if I don't know how?"

"Let me teach you."

I thought of Lovelace's killer and the mastermind of the rooftop burglaries whom I still had to catch. "And that would be when?"

He flashed that wonderful grin that could make me promise or forgive anything. "We'll start in small increments, then expand our lessons once the department has folded."

"Small increments?"

"Finish your burger. I have tickets for Ruth Eckerd Hall at eight. The Canadian Brass are giving a Christmas concert."

I bit into my sandwich, but I was having trouble swallowing. Bill had just declared he wanted to spend the rest of his life with me.

But only if I cleaned up my act.

CHAPTER 14

I slept like a rock straight through the night for the first time since my vacation. I had successfully passed the first hurdle with Bill by thoroughly enjoying myself at the concert that had been part classical music, part camp, and by not mentioning work once. He'd rewarded me by kissing me with more than a little enthusiasm when he'd dropped me off at my condo. I'd almost invited him to spend the night, but decided I'd better take enjoying myself slowly, or I'd blow my circuits.

Suffused with an unfamiliar optimism, I finished my shower and wrapped my head in a towel and my body in a robe before descending the stairs to fix coffee. If Rafferty got a hit on his facial recognition software and Bill's contact led to *Jackpot*, it could be a very good day.

I filled the coffeemaker and had just turned it on when the doorbell rang.

My pulse sped up a bit as I wondered if Bill had

returned early to take up where we had left off last night. Tightening the sash on my robe and adjusting my towel turban, I went to answer it.

Mother stood on the front steps, her back iron-straight and fire flashing in her eyes. Even at seven-thirty in the morning, she was immaculately coiffed and dressed.

"What are you doing here?" My amazement was justified. Mother hadn't set foot in my condo since the day I bought it. Brimming with pride of ownership, I'd invited her over to show off my new home. Unimpressed, she hadn't bothered to return. Not that I'd been twisting her arm with invitations.

She thrust a folded newspaper in my face. "Have you seen this?"

I took the paper, unfolded it and flinched at the three-inch-high headline on the front page of the Pelican Bay edition of the *Times:* Local Woman Arrested In Husband's Murder. And in smaller but not insignificant font beneath: Detective Maggie Skerritt Bags Another Killer.

"How dare you?" Mother was all but frothing at the mouth. "You know Samantha didn't kill Vincent."

I was caught on the horns of a dilemma. If I

agreed with Mother, she'd be storming Shelton's office next. But if I didn't do something to defuse the situation, my already shaky relationship with my mother was *finito*.

"Samantha had means, motive and opportun—"

"Rubbish! Don't spout police jargon at me. Samantha, her girls and Isabelle already have more than they can handle losing Vince. And now you do this."

"I haven't given up trying to find the real killer."

"That doesn't help Samantha or her family now." She snatched the paper from my hand, pivoted on the steps and started down the walk. For the first time, I noticed Hunt's Lincoln in the visitor's space out front with Hunt cowering behind the wheel as if hoping I wouldn't see him.

Halfway down the walk, Mother turned back toward me. When she spoke, her voice was low but perfectly clear. "I've been patient with you, Margaret, in spite of all the trials you've put me through, but this is the final straw. You are no longer a member of this family. And you're not welcome in my house. As far as I'm concerned, I have only one daughter now."

I wanted to defend myself. After all, I'd made

things as easy for Samantha as I could under the circumstances, but I doubted that knowing my feeble efforts would assuage Mother's wrath. I feared anything else I said would only make matters worse.

She turned back toward the car, where Hunt leaped from the driver's seat to open the passenger door for her. Before climbing back in, he faced me with a shrug and a grimace to indicate his helplessness. Mother stared straight ahead and avoided looking at me.

I watched until the Lincoln disappeared, then returned inside.

Lighten up, Bill had warned me.

"Well, Maggie, old girl," I muttered to myself as I stepped inside. "Are we having fun yet?"

I tried giving myself a pep talk on the way to the station. This morning's outburst by Mother was nothing new. I'd known how she felt about me for a long time. Her angry statements had simply made it official.

Then why did it hurt like hell?

With a sigh, I promised myself that the day had to get better. Where else could it go but up? I was rewarded for my optimism when I reached my desk and found a message from Mick Rafferty, head of the county crime lab.

I picked up the phone and dialed his number. "I could really use some good news about now."

"Happy to oblige, Maggie, darlin'. Facial software got a hit on your surveillance video. One bad actor by the name of Leland Kelso. He's in the system. A repeat offender."

"Thanks, Mick. I owe you."

Adler came in as I was pulling up Kelso's rap sheet on the computer.

"Good morning," I said, "and good news." I pointed to the monitor. "This guy made several visits to Bloomberg's without buying squat. And look at this. He lives one street over from Jason McLeod."

"The last robbery was night before last," Adler said. "I doubt Kelso's had time to move the goods. Should I get a search warrant?"

"Absolutely." I scrolled down the page. "And here's the best part. Kelso's has two convictions for robbery. He's served time for both."

"Three strikes and he's out," Adler noted with satisfaction.

"I always wondered about the wording on that law. It should be three strikes and he's in. If we bust him for these rooftop burglaries, Leland Kelso's not going anywhere for a long, long time."

While waiting for our warrant to come through, I put together a photographic lineup that included Kelso's mug shot, then paid a visit to McLeod and Denny in juvenile detention. Prison jumpsuits and a night away from home had reduced their swagger and self-confidence. The boys sat across the table in the interview room looking like the scared little kids they were.

The guard took Denny into a separate interview room, while I talked to Jason.

"We've got your partner in crime," I said. "His picture's in this group I'm going to show you. You'll make things a lot easier for yourself if you give him up."

"He said he'd kill us if we squealed," Jason said.

I shook my head. "This guy's been arrested twice before. When we get him, he's going to be locked up for good. He won't be able to hurt you."

I couldn't help feeling sorry for the boys. Raised without parental supervision or restraints, they'd been easy pickings for a scumbag like Kelso. And, at only twelve years old, they were so heartbreakingly young.

"Okay," McLeod said with reluctance. "Show me the pictures."

Eventually, Jason and Denny both identified Kelso. Before leaving the juvenile detention center, I called Adler to have him add an arrest warrant to the paperwork.

My beeper sounded as I made my way back to the station. After a check with dispatch, I returned Karen Englewood's call. A psychologist, Karen worked at the Pelican Bay Weight Loss Clinic and had almost been Lester Morelli's fourth victim. Adler and I, with some help from Larry, Karen's nineteen-year-old son, had apprehended the killer at Karen's house.

"I know it's short notice," Karen said when she answered, "but how about stopping by for lunch?"

About the same age as me, Karen and I had hit it off immediately during my previous investigation, but I hadn't seen her since Morelli's indictment by the grand jury. In his straight talk about my getting a life, Bill had encouraged me to develop friendships outside the department. With time to kill while waiting for the warrants on Kelso to come through, I took Karen up on her invitation.

Returning to Pelican Bay, I turned off Edgewater Drive onto Windward Lane and parked in front of a large Dutch Colonial home just a few houses in from the waterfront drive.

Karen answered the door on my first ring. An attractive woman with good bones and a great sense of casual style, she was dressed in khaki slacks, a tapestry vest in coordinating colors, a white blouse and cordovan loafers. Her dark hair with its striking streak of gray was pulled back into a French braid. She greeted me with a hug. "It's good to see you, Maggie."

"How's Larry?"

"At work, thank God."

When I'd first met Karen, her son had fallen in with the wrong crowd, taken up booze and pot, and been fired from his job. Just before the attempt on his mother's life, Larry, concerned for her safety after the murder of three of her clients, had cleaned up his act and moved back home.

I smiled at her news. "That's good."

"What's even better," she spoke over her shoulder as I followed her down the hall toward her sunny kitchen, "is that he's also back in school. I don't know how you did it."

I'd had a heart-to-heart talk with Larry during my previous investigation. It's main purpose had been to evaluate him as a suspect, but somehow I'd managed to convince the kid of the error of his ways in his relationship with his mom. The irony of my counseling someone on how to mend fences with his mother hadn't been lost on me.

"Larry's a good kid. You raised him right. He would have come around. I wish I could say that about the kids I've encountered lately."

"Sit—" Karen gestured to a stool at the island in what I called her Galloping Gourmet stage set kitchen "—while I make our salads. What have you been up to? I read in the paper there's been another murder in town."

Karen shredded fresh greens, sliced hard-boiled eggs and carved slices of chicken breast, and I told her briefly about Vince Lovelace, then turned the conversation to Jason McLeod, Richard Denny and Tiffany Harlow.

"There's not much I can do for Jason and Richard at this point," I said. "And that's the frustrating part. For years I've watched Jason sliding into the pit he's in now, and I was helpless to stop him. Judges are loath to take a kid away from his mother, even when she's worthless."

"Did you try Big Brothers?" she asked.

I nodded. "Between Jason and his mom, they scared off every decent guy who tried to help. Jason cleaned out the wallet of his last Big Brother and took his Porsche for a joyride."

After adding a sprinkling of parsley and a garnish of carrot curls and grape tomatoes, Karen slid my salad toward me and passed the dressing. She settled on her own stool and pursed her mouth in thought. "These kids need role models, influences they're not getting at home. And they need them while they're young. At Tiffany's age, for instance. Once they hit their teens, their personalities are pretty much set."

I took a bite of romaine, chewed and swallowed. "With the influx of new residents, all the social services in Pelican Bay are stretched way too thin. Kids fall through the cracks every day."

"Ever thought about starting your own mentoring program?"

I almost choked on a sliver of chicken. "Me? You've got to be kidding. In the first place, I know as much about children as I do about car engines. And in the second, where would I find the time?"

"You mentioned you might be retiring from the department soon."

"That would give me time but not the skills."

"What if I set up a program? I'm only working part-time at the clinic, and, to be honest, I like to keep busy."

I gazed at her in surprise. "You're serious?"

"I don't have to be a rocket scientist to do this," she said with a grin. "Just a psychologist."

"Okay," I conceded, "just for the sake of discussion, supposing you do set up this program. Where do you expect to find mentors?"

She grinned. "Pelican Bay is full of retirees. A lot of them are probably former law enforcement. Maybe they'd like to provide guidance for a child who might otherwise end up on the wrong side of the law."

I thought instantly of Harry Lenkowski, the retired cop who lived in the condo across from Al's Attic. And Bill Malcolm, who loved kids. "If you're willing to look into setting up such a program," I said, "I'll help all I can."

"Good," she said. "Together, maybe we can make a difference."

I dug into my salad and savored the prospect of being proactive instead of reactive where these kids were concerned.

* * *

It was late afternoon before the warrants were issued. Adler and I drove immediately to McLeod's subdivision where earlier I'd posted patrol officers at the ends of Kelso's block to make sure he didn't disappear before we got there.

Accompanied by Johnson and Beaton, Adler and I knocked on Kelso's door at 4:00 p.m.

"Go away," a deep voice shouted through the open jalousies. "I ain't buying nothing."

The dilapidated state of Kelso's house and yard made the McLeod residence look like the Taj Mahal. Whatever profits Kelso had realized from his ill-gotten goods hadn't gone into home improvements. Recalling the cocaine use listed on his rap sheet, I figured most of it had disappeared up his nose.

"Police officers," Adler yelled. "Open the door."

Curses exploded in the room and the sound of frantic movements. A few minutes later, Beaton, who'd been waiting at the back door, escorted a handcuffed Kelso to the front of the house.

A big man in his thirties, Kelso was unwashed and unshaven. Barefoot and limping, he wore only a pair of jeans slung low on his hips.

Beaton grinned. "I knew sandspurs were good for something."

"Yeah," Kelso growled, "if I'd had my shoes, you never would have caught me."

"I wished you'd had them," I said. "Then my officer here could have shot you to keep you from escaping."

I mustered all my self-restraint to curb my temper. Robbing from hardworking folks was bad enough, but training children for his dirty work had been downright evil. "Get him out of here," I ordered Beaton, "before I do something I regret."

Johnson and Beaton took Kelso to the station for booking, and Adler and I remained to search the house. I removed a pair of latex gloves from my pocket, pulled them on, and glanced at Adler. "Ready?"

He nodded. "Let's nail this bastard."

Two hours later we were back at the station with so much evidence that not even an entire cadre of legal eagles would be able to shake our case.

"It's my turn to type up the report," Adler said. "You've put in a long day."

The last thing I wanted was to go home to my empty condo. "It's almost Christmas. Don't you have some shopping to do?"

He grinned. "If we buy any more toys for Jessica, I don't know where we'll hide them. Our bedroom closet already looks like Santa's workshop. You through with your shopping?"

"Haven't bought the first thing." To be honest, I didn't know where to begin. I'd have to ask Miss Manners about the protocol on giving gifts to a mother who's disowned you.

"Then I should be typing this report," Adler said, "so you can hit the mall."

I shook my head. "I might as well work. I don't even have a shopping list yet."

"What are you doing for Christmas this year? Going to your mother's?"

His query caught me by surprise, and to my horror, tears filled my eyes. I blinked rapidly and cleared my throat. "I don't have any plans."

"Why don't you spend Christmas with us?"

"Thanks for asking, but Christmas is for family. I wouldn't want to intrude."

Adler flashed one of his killer smiles. If he used that technique with the women in his life, they had to be putty in his hands. "Maggie, as far as Sharon and I are concerned, you are family. In fact, you should come and bring Bill, too. The more, the merrier."

His words touched me, especially since my own family had just disowned me that very morning. I took a deep breath to keep from tearing up again.

Adler was watching me with his big brown eyes. I studied his face for signs of pity but found only sincerity. Adler had a big heart, and his wife and daughter were lucky to have him.

He must have seen the indecision in my expression, because he added, "You don't have to let me know yet. Just think about it."

"I'll think about it if you'll get out of here and let me finish this report."

He conceded with a nod and another smile. "See you tomorrow. Maybe we'll get a break on Lovelace's killer."

I smiled back at him. "That's all I want for Christmas."

CHAPTER 15

I finished the arrest report on Leland Kelso but couldn't face returning home, where echoes of Mother's angry voice still reverberated through the rooms. Instead, I drove to the marina, parked and made my way through the fog to the *Ten-Ninety-Eight*.

The boisterous bloviating emanating from Bill's television indicated he was watching "The O'Reilly Factor," but he shut off the set as soon as I tapped on the sliding-glass doors.

When he saw me, he opened the door and motioned me inside. "Did you get my message?"

I shook my head. "I haven't been home."

"What's wrong?"

"What makes you think something's wrong?"

"Your eyes are teary, you have this little tic at the corner of your mouth and your hives have hives. Rough day?"

I swallowed a sob, hiccupped and nodded. In an

instant I was enfolded in his arms with my face pressed against his chest. His embrace, coupled with the gentle rocking of the boat, soothed me, and I struggled to regain control of my emotions.

"Want to talk about it?" he asked.

"I hate Christmas."

He pulled me onto the sofa next to him, but didn't let me go. I could feel his gaze searching my face, but I avoided his eyes, afraid I'd give too much away.

"So, this is just a bad case of holiday phobia?"

I nodded.

"You're not on the job now, Margaret. This is Bill, your best bud, you're talking to. If you want to cry, or shout and scream, or lie on the floor and kick your feet, be my guest."

The image of me, wedged in the small space that served as his floor and pitching a tantrum, made me smile, as I'm sure he'd intended.

"That's better," he said. "Now, what's bugging you?"

"It might take less time to tell you what isn't."

"In that case, we need a drink." He rose and headed for the galley. "Have you had dinner?"

I shook my head. "I came straight from the station."

"Could you eat something? I have homemade stew I can heat in the microwave."

I wasn't hungry, but letting him prepare a meal would delay my having to tell all. Within minutes, Bill placed a tray in front of me with a steaming bowl of stew, hot corn muffins and slices of mango with blueberries. The savory smells stimulated my appetite and I dug in.

"How do you do this?" I buttered a muffin and took a bite.

"Cook?"

"I can't even manage to stock my refrigerator."

"Another reason why you should marry me. You need me to keep you from wasting away."

"Fat chance, pun intended." In light of the fragile state of my emotions, marriage was the last thing I wanted to discuss right now.

"I like a woman with meat on her bones." He grinned. "And yours are so wonderfully configured in all the right places."

"If you think by feeding me you'll be able to have your way with me, think again, buster."

"I'm Bill. Buster must be your other guy."

Between the comfort food and Bill's banter, the knot in my stomach was easing. By the time I'd finished the meal, I was relaxed enough to provide a blow-by-blow of Mother's outburst that morning.

"You mustn't blame yourself," he said when I finished.

I laid my head against the back of the sofa and sighed. "Who should I blame, the current administration?"

"I've told you your mother's insecure. She's terrified of what other people think. By washing her hands of you, she thinks she's protecting herself."

"Isn't she?"

Bill shook his head. "She's only demonstrating how pathetic she is, too concerned over her own status to support her daughter."

"I hadn't thought of it that way."

"Because you're too close to the situation to be objective."

"Her attitude still hurts."

"Of course it does." He'd carried the tray back to the galley and returned to sit next to me. He put his arms around me and held me close. "But your friends know the truth."

Realizing how much he meant to me, I snuggled into his embrace. But the situation was heading in a dangerous direction, one my feelings were too raw to handle. I diverted the conversation with a full account of Kelso's arrest.

"So that's one case, at least, that's closed," I concluded.

"Damn, you're good, Margaret."

"As much as I hate to admit it, technology made the difference in this investigation. I'd still be in the dark without Rafferty's facial recognition software."

Bill shook his head. "Mug shots and shoe leather would have brought Kelso down eventually. Rafferty's help just speeded up the process."

"What did you find out from the boat mechanic?"

"That was the message I left you. Nada on *Jackpot*. But the mechanic did give me the name of a guy who specializes in painting and detailing cigarette boats. If the painter doesn't know the boat and its owner, then I'll start checking the distributors."

"Where's this painter located?"

Bill nodded. "A dry dock near Davis Island."

"What about jurisdiction?"

"I figured you could call Abe Mackley and fill him in?"

"Mackley's still with the Tampa P.D.?"

"Due to retire in the spring."

"I'll call him in the morning," I said, "and fill him in on our case. Then I'll go with you to question the painter. We have to find that boat. If its owner is a random killer, we're running out of time before he strikes again." I stood to leave.

"Stay here tonight," Bill said.

As much as I wanted to comply, I shook my head. "You're just feeling sorry for me."

He pushed to his feet, took my face in his hands and looked into my eyes. "I know exactly what I'm feeling, and, believe me, Margaret, it's not sorry."

The next morning Bill drove me back to my condo and called Abe Mackley while I showered and dressed. Our relationship had taken a new turn when we'd slept together last night, and I felt as if I'd stepped off the edge of a cliff and still hadn't hit bottom. I was moving toward commitment, and I was scared out of my mind. Although I was warming to the idea of marriage, of working and growing old with Bill, I was too rusty at relationships, I feared I'd bungle things badly. One look at my disconnection from my own family proved how inept I was. Bill's friendship was the most precious part of my life. He was the only person who accepted me without judgment, always told me the truth, but with kindness, and treated me with unlimited generosity of spirit. I was still terrified that by taking that final step to matrimony, I would jeopardize all that was good in our relationship.

Earlier this morning, Bill had pooh-poohed my fears. "We'll always be friends, Margaret. But added to that, we'll have the pleasure of waking up to each other every morning, spending the better part of our days together, and holding each other every night while we sleep. I want to grow old with you. What's not to like about that?"

"I like it, all right, too much. But what if I mess it up somehow? What if I can't learn to lighten up? What if you get sick of me?"

He'd pulled me against him in the wide bed that filled the cabin and the heat of his skin had warmed me. "How long have we been friends, Margaret?"

"Twenty-two years."

"That's a pretty good track record, don't you think?"

"But we didn't have the hurdle of marriage."

"It doesn't have to be a hurdle."

"I don't know the first thing about being married."

He grew still and didn't say anything for a moment. "I've had experience," he finally said, "but since my first wife walked out on me, maybe you figure I'm not a good risk."

"That's not true!" I sat upright and stared at him. "Tricia couldn't take the pressure of being a cop's wife. That was her weakness, not yours."

"I could have changed jobs," he said. "Chosen a career that was safer and didn't scare her so much."

"And denied who you are? You'd have been so miserable, your marriage wouldn't have survived. Besides, you were a cop when Tricia married you. She knew what she was in for."

"Maybe," Bill said. "But I don't blame her for leaving. She went to pieces after that domestic call when I almost bought the farm. Continual exposure to that kind of stress is a lot to ask of anyone. My biggest regret is that she took Melanie so far away."

"Tricia still loved you," I said. "If she'd lived where you could visit regularly and she'd had to see you often, she could never have made the break."

"What about you?" he asked.

"What about me?"

"Do *you* love me?"

I searched frantically for a flippant remark to defuse the intensity, but my mind went blank. I finally spoke from the heart. "God help me, Malcolm, I've loved you from the day we met."

Relief cascaded across his face. "You know I love you, Margaret. Between us, we should be able to figure this marriage thing out."

He'd kissed me, effectively squelching further protests. Then, while I'd slept a little longer, he'd showered and fixed our breakfast.

Back at my condo and dressed for the day, I went downstairs where Bill waited in the living room and put in a call to Adler.

"I'm going to Lovelace's funeral this morning," Adler said. "It's at the Episcopal Church then burial at Pilgrims' Rest."

We'd agreed earlier that, under the circumstances, I should avoid the services. I didn't trust my mother not to make a scene if she spotted me.

"I'll be on the lookout," Adler added, "for any suspicious strangers. Afterward, I'll do another canvass of the Lovelace neighborhood. See if anyone remembers something they haven't told us."

"Or has sighted that cigarette boat again," I reminded him. "Bill and I are going to Tampa to try to track it down."

"The forensics accountants should finish their audit of Lovelace's books today," Adler said. "That will tell us if there's a money problem that could have precipitated Lovelace's murder."

"I'll check with you this afternoon," I said, and hung up.

If the cigarette boat turned out to be a dead end and Lovelace's books were clean, unless Adler turned up something or someone suspicious at the funeral or on his canvass, our investigation was dead in the water.

Pinellas, a small peninsula on Florida's West Coast, bounded by St. Pete on the south and Tarpon Springs at the north, is the state's most densely populated county. In my lifetime, the area had changed from an agricultural paradise of citrus groves and dairy farms rimmed by white sand beaches to a solid mass of residential and business districts, wall-to-wall concrete and asphalt. Roads were constantly clogged with traffic, especially from Thanksgiving to Easter, when the influx of tourists was at its height.

Making our way from Pelican Bay to the Tampa

causeway took a hair-raising hour. With a preponderance of drivers who were often elderly and frequently lost on unfamiliar roadways, I literally took my life in my hands every time I stepped into a car and hit the streets. Bill, who was both experienced and cautious, was driving, but I still found myself clutching the armrest until my knuckles whitened and pressing my feet against the floorboards, a nervous reaction to idiots on the roads.

The drive across the four-lane causeway, a thin spit of land that traversed Tampa Bay, showcased Florida in all its glory. On both sides of the roadway stretched clear, blue-green water, sparkling in the sun. Palm trees and oleanders separated the asphalt from the strips of beach, and a magnificent cloudless sky arched overhead. With the Northeast crippled by a blizzard and below-freezing temperatures, I understood why people flocked to Florida like migratory birds.

I understood, but I wished they'd stayed home.

We left the causeway, passed Tampa International Airport, and entered Interstate 275, the main artery through the city. After only a few terrifying miles of high-speed gridlock, we exited toward Davis Island and the marina where Bill's contact worked.

"Makes you glad you don't have to work in this traffic every day, doesn't it?" Bill said.

"It wasn't this bad fifteen years ago."

He laughed. "Hell, it wasn't this bad two years ago."

We parked near the marina and walked to the dry dock. A young man in a paint-stained T-shirt and shorts sat on an overturned 30-gallon drum, his face, exposed by a spattered ball cap worn backward, raised to the sun. When he saw us approach, he set his coffee mug aside and walked to meet us.

"Need some boat work done?" he asked.

"Steve at Rocky Point Boat Repair sent us," Bill said. "Are you Smitty?"

"Yeah," he replied with a goofy smile. The kid didn't seem too bright, as if he'd spent too many hours inhaling paint fumes. "Who wants to know?"

I showed my shield. "Maggie Skerritt, Pelican Bay police. This is Bill Malcolm. We have some questions if you have the time."

His grin faded with his prospect for profit and his expression turned wary. "What's this about?"

"We're trying to locate a cigarette boat," I said. "Its owner might have witnessed a crime, and we'd like to talk to him."

"Unfortunately," Bill added, "all we know is the name of the boat."

"*Jackpot*," I said. "You ever worked on a boat with that name?"

"Is the owner in trouble?" Smitty asked.

"Right now, he's just a possible witness," I repeated. "You know the boat?"

"Sure," Smitty said. "I painted the name on it myself."

"Recently?"

He scratched his head with a paint-covered finger. "I can't remember, exactly."

"You keep records?" Bill asked.

"Yeah," he said, then grinned sheepishly. "Well, sort of."

"You mind looking up this boat," I said, "and telling us the owner's name and address?"

"I won't be getting him into trouble, will I? That would be bad for business."

"If he's in any trouble, it's his own doing," I assured him. "Besides, we don't have to tell him how we found him."

The kid's goofy look brightened at my assurance. He jerked his head toward a small shed at the edge of the dry dock. "I keep my records in there."

We followed Smitty inside the tiny enclosure, where there was barely room for the three of us, and I discovered that Smitty had used the term "keeping records" loosely. He had no desk, only a wooden shelf nailed across one side of the shed. On it were haphazard stacks of papers and a few spindles crammed with invoices. So many cans of paint and varnish crowded the structure, I was tempted to roll a hazmat team.

"This'll just take a minute," Smitty assured us.

Bill and I exchanged doubtful glances.

Twenty minutes later Smitty discovered the invoice he needed at the bottom of the last spindle he'd searched. "Here it is! *Jackpot!*" he shouted. He gave a chuckle that matched his goofy expression and looked to see if we'd shared his joke.

"And the winner is?" Bill said.

"Huh?"

I guessed Smitty's sparkling repartee only extended so far.

"Who's the owner?" I asked.

He handed me the color-smeared invoice. I didn't see how the kid turned a profit at the rate he wasted paint.

"*Jackpot*'s owned by Rayburn Price," I said. "Address listed is on Dundee."

"That's off Westshore Boulevard," Bill said. "Lots of canals that connect to the bay in that area."

I returned the invoice to Smitty. "Thanks for your help and your time."

"No problemo," the kid said. "And if you ever need a cigarette boat painted, I'm your man."

Bill drove us into downtown Tampa to One Police Center on Franklin Street and dropped me off to meet with Mackley while he searched for a parking space. We were hoping Mackley would help us dig up info on our suspect.

Before entering the building I stopped for a moment at the police memorial, a tribute to those who have made the ultimate sacrifice for the citizens of Tampa. Instead of a statue of an officer as a monument, the silhouette of a policeman had been cut away from the polished stone, leaving an empty space, a symbol of the hole that the death of an officer leaves in the hearts of the people who loved him. Or her. One of the department's most recent fatalities was a female officer gunned down during a bank robbery in 2001.

The memorial reminded me to be cautious. Rayburn Price might simply be an innocent boater, a voyeur at worst. Or he could be a cold-blooded killer. Whatever the case, I didn't want to be a statistic. On average, a police officer is killed in the line of duty every fifty-two hours in this country, and every year 65,000 criminal assaults, resulting in more than 23,000 injuries, are committed against officers. Funny how any spurious charge of police brutality always made the news, but these statistics were rarely given.

At any rate, the memorial served not only as a reminder of those we'd lost, but also as a warning to those who still worked the streets. When the time came to make an arrest, I'd approach my suspect with caution. And plenty of backup.

After parking the car, Bill joined me and we went inside to meet Mackley. An old friend who'd started with us on patrol before making detective, Abe looked enough like Sipowicz on "NYPD Blue" to be his body double. He led us to his office in the Investigations department and offered us seats and coffee.

We passed on the coffee and I filled Abe in on what we'd learned about Rayburn Price.

"Let me see what I can find." He sat at his desk

and let his fingers fly over the keyboard of his computer, a considerably newer model than the antique on my own desk. After a few minutes he shook his head. "Rayburn's not in the system. Not even a parking ticket. Your boy is clean."

"Could he be using an alias?" I asked.

"It's possible, but unless he's been arrested under the alias, we'd have no way of knowing about it. Let me check a few data banks, see what else I can find on your boy."

Mackley's pudgy fingers were getting a workout, but also results. "Got him," he said. "Rayburn Price on Dundee. He's listed in the city business directory. Works as an underwriter for Orange Belt Life Insurance Company. They're in a building just two blocks over."

"Life insurance?" Bill and I said in unison.

"Your vic have a policy?" Mackley asked.

"The mother of all policies," I said. "Ten million double indemnity. But his wife's the beneficiary."

"Maybe she has a sweet deal going with Price," Abe said. "He knocks off the husband and they split the pot."

"Can I borrow your phone?" I asked.

Abe shoved the telephone toward me and a quick call to Hunt confirmed that the policy he'd written on Lovelace had been with Orange Belt Life.

"You have the paperwork on that policy handy?" I asked.

"Hold on," Hunt said. "I'll have my secretary get the file."

A few minutes later Hunt was back on the line. "I've got the file in front of me. What do you need to know?"

"Who was the underwriter?"

The sound of pages turning traveled through the line and Hunt gave a grunt that indicated he'd found what he was looking for. "Underwriter was Rayburn Price. Does that help?"

"Yeah, thanks, Hunt."

"Margaret?" he said before I could hang up.

"Yes?"

"I'm sorry about, uh, you know."

He was referring to Mother, who was the last person I wanted to discuss at the moment. "It's okay, Hunt. I understand."

Bill and Mackley looked at me when I hung up the receiver.

"Well?" Bill said.

265

"Price was the underwriter on Lovelace's policy," I told them with a sinking feeling in my gut. "If we can establish a tie between him and Samantha, it looks as if I arrested the right person after all."

CHAPTER 16

Rather than drive two blocks and search for another parking spot, Bill and I walked to the Orange Belt Life Insurance building. As a professional courtesy, I'd invited Abe to come along, but he'd declined, asking me to fill him in later on what I learned. I'd seen the stack of case files teetering like the Leaning Tower of Pisa on the corner of his desk. He had plenty of work of his own to keep him busy without dogging our steps.

At the insurance company's receptionist's desk, we asked to see the head of underwriting and were directed to a fourth-floor office with wide windows overlooking the Hillsborough River and the minarets of the University of Tampa. The name on the desk read Virginia O'Connell. The woman behind the desk was in her fifties, dressed in a navy-blue power suit with a white silk blouse. She wore her dark hair pulled back from her face, and her eyes, framed by silver glasses, regarded us with suspicion.

"Why are the Pelican Bay Police interested in Orange Belt Life?" she asked.

"It's just routine," I assured her. "One of your policyholders was murdered in my jurisdiction. I need to check out the beneficiary on his policy."

I already knew the beneficiary, but I figured if I started nosing around about Rayburn Price right off the bat, Miss Prim-and-Proper would close up tighter than a night-blooming cereus at sunrise.

"Of course," Ms. O'Connell said. "And what is the name of the deceased?"

"Vincent Lovelace."

She turned to her computer and typed in the name. "He has a ten-million-dollar policy with his wife Samantha as his beneficiary."

I made a show of writing down the information and was about to broach the subject of Price when she spoke again. "And another ten-million-dollar policy with Reginald Purdy as beneficiary."

"Reginald Purdy?" I tried to cover my surprise. "Are you sure?"

The look she shot me would have withered a weaker woman. "Of course."

"Do you have an address for Purdy?"

"Just a post-office box in Longboat Key." She gave me the number and zip code.

"Has the payment been made to Purdy?"

She checked her computer again. "The claim form came in yesterday. The check should go out tomorrow. And your other question?"

"Who was the underwriter on the Purdy policy?"

She arched her eyebrows. "Why do you ask?"

"Just routine." I gave her my warmest smile. "You know how bosses are if you don't get everything right."

"Rayburn Price was the underwriter on both policies," she said. "But that's not unusual. Mr. Price is one of our best underwriters. He's been with us fifteen years."

"And the agent of record on the Purdy policy?" I must have absorbed more of Hunt's mind-numbing monologues than I'd realized. I was spouting insurance jargon better than the Geico gekko.

O'Connell sighed and turned back to her monitor. "Agent of record on both policies is Huntington Yarborough."

Again I managed to keep my surprise from showing. "Would it be possible to get copies of the paperwork on those policies?"

The thin set of her mouth revealed her annoyance, but her words were courteous. "Of course."

She buzzed an intercom and, when her secretary appeared, requested the copies.

While we waited, Bill worked his charm. "You must be a valued member of this company."

At first, Ms. O'Connell was skeptical. "What makes you say that?"

He nodded toward the windows. "I suspect a lot of your co-workers envy you this office with such a fantastic view."

It was good cop/bad cop, and Bill was as good as they get. By the time the secretary returned with the copies I'd requested, Bill was oohing and aahing over pictures of Ms. O'Connell's grandchildren.

The smile she bestowed on us when we left was infinitely warmer than her initial greeting had been.

On the way back from Tampa, we stopped at a Red Lobster on the east end of the causeway. With the lunch crowd gone and the early diners not yet arrived, with the exception of an elderly couple in a corner booth, we had the restaurant to ourselves.

We requested a booth in a corner opposite the

old folks and gave our order to the waitress. I stared at the folder Ms. O'Connell had given me.

"Go ahead," Bill said. "Take a look."

"I'm gathering my nerve."

"For what?"

"In case Hunt's involved."

Bill blinked in surprise. "Why would you think your brother-in-law is in on this?"

I shared Hunt's proposed book plot about an insurance agent who had planted fake beneficiaries and raked in the dough when the insureds died.

"That doesn't mean he's involved," Bill said. "I'm sure every agent in the business is aware of those kinds of scams."

"You're right," I said. "Besides, Hunt wouldn't have the balls to pull this off unless Caroline egged him on, and my sister considers crime socially unacceptable."

I flipped open the folder and pulled out the application for Lovelace's policy. Hunt's bold signature in fat black strokes jumped out at me from the bottom of the last page. I turned to the final page of the second app with Purdy as the beneficiary. Hunt's signature appeared there, too.

Exactly the same. Too much the same.

I grunted in surprise.

"What have you got?" Bill asked.

I detached the final pages of each app, overlapped them, and held them up to the light streaming through the window. The signatures were an exact match. "Someone traced Hunt's signature."

"Let me see those," Bill said.

I slid the apps across the table and he scanned them quickly. "The app for the second policy has the same date as the first. You suppose Hunt's secretary has a stamp with his signature?"

"Just when I thought things couldn't get worse," I said with a terrible foreboding. "Can you imagine Mother's wrath when I start investigating her favorite son-in-law?"

Before Bill could reply, my beeper sounded. I looked at the number. "It's Ms. O'Connell at Orange Belt Life."

With my head still spinning at the prospect of Hunt's involvement, I hurried to the phone in the lobby and punched in the number of the head underwriter.

"Detective Skerritt," she said in a low voice that was almost a whisper, "thank God, I reached you. You'd better get back here as quick as you can."

"What's wrong?"

"I did some snooping on my own after you left. Did a computer search of all the policies Ray Price has underwritten."

"And?"

"He's underwritten six other multimillion-dollar policies that name Reginald Purdy as beneficiary."

"Is Huntington Yarborough the agent?" I held my breath for her answer.

"No, there are six different agents scattered all over the state. Each insured has another policy, apparently written at the same time, to other beneficiaries as well as the one to Purdy. It's highly irregular. I thought you'd want to know."

"I'll come straight back to your office," I said. "Make me copies, please, but, whatever you do, don't mention this investigation to anyone, especially Rayburn Price."

I returned to the booth just as the waitress was serving our meal.

"What's up?" Bill said.

"We have to go. This case just got a whole lot more complicated."

After gathering copies of the other policies from Ms. O'Connell, Bill and I returned to One Police

Center. Abe provided an empty desk and computer access, and we went to work.

Of the seven named insureds on the life policies, four, including Lovelace, were dead. All had been healthy, rich men in their thirties. Two of the deaths were listed as accidental drownings. A third, a real-estate entrepreneur who'd lived on Captiva Island, had been murdered in what appeared to have been a botched boat accident. That case was still open.

We were not surprised to find that Reginald Purdy, the beneficiary on all seven policies, did not exist. Apparently Rayburn Price had used the info on the bona fide applications to create fake apps for additional policies that left the money to Purdy.

"So Price leaves no trail," I said. "All he needs is fake ID, available on any street corner, to rent a post-office box and open a bank account in Purdy's name. He deposits the checks from the insurance company, then transfers the money into his own accounts. As long as the deaths of the insureds appear accidental, nobody's the wiser."

"But our boy slipped up," Bill said. "Eventually, they always do, in spite of the TV and movie myths of the perfect crime."

I nodded. "Lovelace was supposed to have

drowned after the blow to his head. If Price hadn't had to hold him under, we might have suspected foul play, but we couldn't have proved Vincent's death wasn't accidental."

Abe offered to place Price under surveillance until I could set up my own network, and Bill and I returned to Pelican Bay. Adler was waiting at my condo when we drove in.

He followed us inside. "Sorry, Maggie, but I came up empty today. No new leads."

"It's okay," I said with a smile, and brought him up to speed on what Bill and I had uncovered.

"Are you going to bring Price in?" Adler asked.

"Oh, yeah," I said, "but first I'm going to catch him with his hand in the till."

Adler raised his eyebrows. "How?"

"Ms. O'Connell said the check to Purdy goes out tomorrow. It should hit the Longboat Key post office the next day. That gives us tomorrow to contact the Longboat Key P.D. and set our trap."

"Collar him when he picks up the mail?" Adler asked.

Bill shook his head. "There's a bank just across the parking lot from the post office. My guess is that Reginald Purdy has an account there."

"We'll check with the bank manager tomorrow

to make certain that's where his account is," I said. "If so, we'll nab him when he endorses the check."

"And if not?" Adler asked.

"We'll tail him until he stops for a deposit."

"What about the other guys?" Adler said.

"What other guys?" Bill asked.

"Price's prospective victims."

"We'll notify them tomorrow, too," I said, "to put them on their guard, but I doubt Price will make another move before he has the money from his most recent kill in the bank."

"Guess you've just about wrapped up Shelton's Christmas gift," Adler said.

"I'm not doing this for Shelton," I said.

"But you know how it is, Maggie." A boyish grin split Adler's face. "If Shelton ain't happy, ain't none of us happy."

"None of us will be happy when Ulrich shuts down the department," I said, "but we might as well get this killer and go out with a bang."

CHAPTER 17

Two days later the Tampa detectives watching Price called to inform us that the underwriter hadn't gone to work that day but had left his house and driven south on the Sunshine Skyway, so my team moved into place. With Adler watching the Longboat Key post-office box, Bill keeping an eye on Price's car in the parking lot, and me waiting in the bank lobby, Rayburn Price didn't have a chance.

I had studied Price's DMV mug shot and the photos taken by Abe's surveillance team until Price's face was as familiar as my own. Bill gave me a heads-up on the radio when Price strolled into the post office. With a nod to alert the bank manager and my Longboat Key P.D. counterpart, who waited together in the manager's glass-enclosed office, I took a seat on a vinyl-covered sofa next to the teller line and waited.

Within minutes Price, a tall man in his forties

and dressed in expensive casual clothes, sauntered into the bank. He didn't look like a killer but an average guy running an errand. He stopped at a desk near the entrance, filled out a deposit slip, endorsed a check and stepped to the end of the teller line.

While Price waited for the two people ahead of him to finish their transactions, Adler came into the bank and paused at the desk Price had vacated. Through the double-glass entrance doors, I could see Bill Malcolm, leaning on a car in a handicapped parking spot and watching the front doors.

Price was a cool customer. After all, he'd apparently pulled this stunt several times before and had no reason to suspect any problems. He stood at ease, humming softly under his breath, as if he had all the time in the world. When he reached the head of the line, he handed the young female teller his paperwork.

"Good morning, Mr. Purdy," she said with a bright commercial smile. "Nice to see you again."

"It's a beautiful day." His voice was warm, deep and pleasant, not what you'd expect a killer to sound like.

"Yes, it is. The kind Florida's famous for." With quick efficiency, she processed his deposit, printed out his receipt and handed it to him. "You have a nice day."

He folded the receipt, tucked it in the pocket of his golf shirt and turned toward the door. But he didn't get far, because I had stood and blocked his way.

"Excuse me," he said.

"Of course," I replied with a smile, but didn't budge. "By the way, have you heard about the new policy?"

"A new banking policy?"

I nodded. "A safety precaution."

By now Price was looking around as if not wanting to cause a scene. His brow furrowed over his strange amber-colored eyes.

"Do you work here?" he asked.

"Only for today." Out of the corner of my eye, I saw Adler moving toward us. "That policy I mentioned? I'm here to insure that you get life—if you're lucky. Florida also has the death penalty, you know."

His pupils widened with comprehension, but before he could take a step, Adler was on one side of him, the cop from Longboat Key on the other, and Bill blocked the entrance like a linebacker.

"You're under arrest for the murder of Vincent

Lovelace," I said with great satisfaction, and read him his rights.

Within minutes Price was in cuffs in the back of my car. Adler rode beside him and Bill sat in the passenger seat next to me. During the hour-and-a-half trip back to Pelican Bay, Price didn't say a word.

I'd called Shelton from the bank to let him know we'd picked up Price, so the crowd of media mobbing the lawn outside the sally port when we returned to the station didn't surprise me. Shelton had made sure we'd have plenty of witnesses to the perp walk. Price tried to hide his face from the cameras, but with his hands cuffed behind him, his efforts were futile.

As soon as Price had been booked, Shelton shouted down the hall, "Skerritt, I want you in the briefing room. Now!"

I hurried to the room where Shelton had set up an impromptu press conference. At the front of the room, he sat at a table that bristled with microphones. In the glare of camera flashes and television lights, he motioned me to a seat beside him.

"I'm happy to announce that we have Rayburn Price, a suspect in the Lovelace murder, in custody," he announced. "He was apprehended by my officers earlier today in Longboat Key."

A perky young woman from WFLA raised her hand. "But you've already arrested Mrs. Lovelace. Is Price an accomplice?"

"No, Price acted on his own," Shelton said.

"So you made a mistake," the reporter continued, "when you arrested Mrs. Lovelace?"

Shelton squirmed like a fish that had been gaffed. He'd ordered me to arrest Samantha, despite my insistence that she was innocent. If I told that to the press, he'd look like an idiot.

I considered for an instant the infinite satisfaction of seeing Shelton's incompetence exposed on every television set in the Bay area. But I couldn't bring myself to do it. The department was on death watch and losing his job was punishment enough.

"We arrested Mrs. Lovelace as a feint," I said, "so the real killer wouldn't know we were on to him."

"And she was okay with that?" a husky correspondent from the *Times* asked.

I improvised. "Mrs. Lovelace's primary wish is to see her husband's killer brought to justice. She was willing to do everything in her power to that end."

Neither Shelton nor I told the press about Price's other victims. Those were ongoing investigations that even Shelton knew better than to compromise. He answered a few more questions, then fled to his office with me in tow.

"You did good work, Skerritt," he said after he'd closed the door.

"I had plenty of help. Adler, Bill Malcolm and the Tampa and Longboat Key departments." But not from Shelton. He'd been an impediment from the git-go.

Shelton sank into his desk chair like a defeated foe. "It's good to go out on top."

"Go out? Are you firing me?"

His eyes were dark hollows. "We've all been fired, Maggie. The council voted an hour ago to disband the department the first of February. The sheriff's office takes over then."

Even though I had seen it coming, the reality hurt like hell. "I thought the citizens were supposed to vote."

Shelton shook his head. "The council decided that the savings to the city are so great, they'd be fiscally irresponsible not to push forward with the change. There's a citizens' group gathering petitions for a referendum, but by the time they've jumped through the necessary legal hoops, they'll be too late. Once the department's disbanded, it would cost millions to reinstate it, and the taxpayers won't go for the expense. That's what happened in Dunedin, remember?"

I thought of Adler, Johnson, Beaton, Darcy, Kyle and all the other members of the department who'd been my only family for the past fifteen years. "Do the others know?"

Shelton shook his head. "As soon as the media clear out, I'm calling a meeting to announce the council's decision."

"Helluva Christmas present," I said, and left quickly so he'd think I hadn't seen the tears in his eyes.

CHAPTER 18

I'd never been fond of Christmas, and this year the holidays held even more bittersweet moments than in years past.

The department's party at the Adlers, our last official gathering, had been tough on everyone. Johnson and Beaton had drunk too much, Lenny Jacobs had made a farewell speech that had us all crying in our eggnog, and Adler had announced that he'd be resigning the first of the year to take the job he'd been offered with the Clearwater department. Everyone had promised to stay in touch, but we'd all been painfully aware that nothing would be the same. Like a household broken by divorce, we'd go our separate ways and never really be a family again.

And I soon discovered that catching Vincent Lovelace's killer had been no help in restoring me to Mother's good graces.

"I'm sorry, Margaret," Caroline had said when she called to congratulate me on Price's arrest. "You know how she is."

"I embarrassed her in front of her friends, the unpardonable sin," I admitted.

"Hunt thinks you're brilliant, even if you have stolen his thunder on the book he was planning to write."

"Truth is stranger than fiction." Having an actual conversation with my sister was also strange, like sailing through uncharted waters.

"We want you and Bill to come over for supper Christmas Eve," Caroline said. "A nice quiet evening with just the four of us."

Now I knew I was dreaming. "You're sure? I don't want you on the outs with Mother for my sake."

"We're sisters, Margaret. And Christmas is for families."

Her loyalty, especially in the face of Mother's disapproval, touched me. "I'll check with Bill and let you know."

The following Saturday morning, Bill called a few minutes past seven. "Can I pick you up in an hour? I have something to show you."

"You sound amazingly cheerful for so early in the morning."

"Did I wake you?"

"No, I've been up a while. With my cases closed, I've finally been able to get some decent sleep. And with the department soon to be kaput, I'm looking forward to more nights of uninterrupted rest."

"Dress warm," he said with a smile in his voice. "It's beginning to feel like Christmas out there."

A check of the Weather Channel after I hung up indicated highs only in the fifties with a wind chill factor in the thirties, so I tugged on jeans and a bulky sweater and was ready when Bill arrived precisely an hour later.

"Where are we going?" I asked as I followed him to his car.

"Not far."

With his blue eyes twinkling and his self-satisfied expression, he was operating in his it's-a-secret mode, so further questions were useless. I climbed into his car, fastened my seat belt and prepared to be surprised.

He turned north on Edgewater and drove past the marina into the heart of downtown and parked in front of a two-story building on the corner across from SunTrust Bank. The old brick building there, built in 1905, had been the original bank before their new quarters were erected across the street. Now the old bank's lower floor held a coffeeshop and bookstore.

Once out of the car, however, Bill bypassed the bookstore entrance and directed me to accompany him down the side street. At the back of the building was another entrance. Bill opened that door and motioned me ahead of him.

I stepped inside and climbed the steep stairs to the second floor.

"These used to be law and medical offices when this building was first built," Bill said.

"What's up here now?"

We'd reached the top of the stairs. Bill pointed to a door on the left, where daylight poured through the frosted glass of the top half of a door. "That's a graphic design studio. And down that hall to your right is an accounting office. But we're going straight ahead."

I preceded him down the long hall, then moved aside while he opened a door also topped with frosted glass. He swung the door wide, went in and pulled me inside. "Well, what do you think?"

It was a remarkable space, open and airy with tall sash windows that reached to the top of the ten-foot ceilings and flooded the rooms with light. There was a smaller room immediately to the left, a large open room on the corner of the building that overlooked both downtown and the marina, and a tiny kitchen and bathroom on the right. The heart-pine floors glistened in the sunlight and, even empty, the rooms were cheerful and bright.

"Are you planning to rent this?" I asked.

"Depends on whether you approve."

I hesitated. The space was attractive, but definitely too small for a household of two. "You're the one who'd be living here."

"I don't intend to live here."

He chuckled at my dumbfounded expression, dug into his pocket and handed me a business card. "I was playing around on the computer yesterday and made this up."

The card, decorated in the upper right-hand corner with the silhouette of a pelican, read, "Pelican Bay Investigations" with the Main Street address of the building in which we stood printed beneath. In the bottom left-hand corner, he'd printed my name, in the right, his.

"This is our new office," he said, and added hastily, "but only if you like it."

"I love it." I glanced around, imagining spending my days in this sunny space, working with Bill. "But can we afford it?"

He quoted the price the real-estate agent had given him.

"Why so low?" I asked.

"No elevator," he said. "Lots of businesses don't want a place without one. I figure we can make do, arrange to meet elderly or handicapped clients somewhere else if necessary."

My footsteps echoed in the emptiness as I walked around the suite from room to room, checking the view from every window, flushing the toilet in the bathroom, turning on the faucets in the kitchen. My old life as a detective was coming to an end, unless I wanted to relocate to another department in another city. But I loved Pelican Bay and didn't want to leave. The time had come to stop looking back and look ahead.

I glanced up to find Bill watching me with a

CHARLOTTE DOUGLAS

worried expression. "I love it," I said again. "Let's take it."

With a whoop, he grabbed me in a bear hug and swung me off my feet. When he finally set me down, I was dizzy, both from spinning and apprehension over whether I'd made the right decision.

"We'll need office furniture," I said.

"No problem. Secondhand stuff will work fine for us, and we can get it for a song. I'm more worried about a secretary."

I had a brilliant idea. "What about Darcy Wilkins?"

"The dispatcher?"

I nodded. "Support staff will have a hard time finding new positions. Darcy will need a job, and she's both reliable and discreet."

"So, if Darcy's willing," Bill said with a happy grin, "we have everything we need."

"Clients would be helpful."

"Ah, Margaret, have faith. If we build it, they will come."

Christmas Eve, Bill and I returned to my condo after having dinner with Caroline and Hunt.

Hunt had been fascinated by the details of Rayburn Price's murders.

"So he was a serial killer," Hunt said.

I nodded. "But, unlike most serial killers, he didn't murder for the thrill. Just the money. Our investigation found that he was moving the millions he'd scammed from life insurance to a bank in the Caymans. Apparently, once he'd killed and collected on his three remaining victims, he planned to leave the country and disappear."

"Is he being charged with the murder in Captiva, too?" Caroline asked.

"Yep," Bill said. "His prints were found all over the boat where his victim, killed weeks before Lovelace, died in a faked accident. But Price's prints weren't in the data base then, and the Lee County investigators couldn't identify him until he'd been arrested and fingerprinted in Pelican Bay."

"So Price isn't going anywhere," Hunt said.

"Except Raiford," I said. "The state attorney's office will ask for the death penalty in the Lovelace murder. And charges have yet to be brought in the other murders."

"Poor Samantha," Caroline said. "This will be a sad Christmas for her and the girls."

Bill quickly changed the subject. "Margaret and I need to talk to you about insurance, Hunt."

Hunt's expression brightened. "What kind?"

"We're going to need a business policy."

The conversation shifted to our new venture, and by the time we'd finished our meal and two bottles of excellent wine, I was surprised to find that I was enjoying myself.

Back at my condo, I switched on the television, where a local cable station was running uninterrupted footage of a fireplace, complete with burning logs and Christmas stockings, accompanied by Christmas carols. Even if my living room had had a fireplace, it would have been too warm for a fire. Bill opened the sliders to the patio to the southwest breeze and the crisp smell of salt and sea.

Earlier in the week, Bill had insisted that we get a tree, a real tree, and the pungent scent of fir mixed with the tangy aroma from the sound. I'd owned no lights or ornaments, so Bill had volunteered to shop for trimmings and to decorate. He was a man who loved surprises. I had returned home a few days ago to find the fir draped with white twinkle lights, blue-and-green silk balls the color of the sea, sand dollars and starfish bleached and dried to a creamy white, and garlands made from tiny shells.

"It goes with your Florida tourist decor," he'd explained, looking immensely proud.

He'd always teased me that my condo had the same decor as a suite at the Pelican Bay Hilton on the beach, but I loved the soothing sea colors. And his tree was a perfect fit, not the garish intrusion I'd expected.

"What?" I'd asked. "No flamingos?"

"You can have them if you like."

I had shaken my head. "It's perfect, just as it is. Thank you."

With only the glow from the fire projected on the television screen and the twinkle lights on the tree, we sat on the sofa and listened to the medley of carols.

"I haven't felt this relaxed in a long time," I said.

"All that wine at dinner."

I thought for a moment. "It's more than that. I feel…content."

Bill put his arms around me and tugged me closer. "Me, too. But there's one thing missing."

I pulled back and looked at him. "We have the tree, the fire, the carols. What else is there?"

He released me to fish in the pocket of his slacks and withdraw a small velvet-covered box. "Your Christmas present."

He flipped open the box and took out a delicate yellow gold band set with three aquamarines, elegant in its simplicity. "Will you marry me, Margaret?"

My eyes filled with tears at the beauty and thoughtfulness of his choice. He'd selected my birthstone, knowing that a diamond solitaire held too many memories of Greg and that I'd want a ring that reminded me only of Bill. "It's beautiful."

He started to speak but had to clear the emotion from his throat. "There are three stones, one for our past, one for the present, and the third for our future together."

"I don't know what to say."

"*Yes* would be good."

"I know, but I'm scared."

"Scared of me?"

I shook my head. "Everything's changing so fast.

Losing my job, starting a new business. I'm terrified that if we throw marriage into the mix right now, we're asking for trouble."

He smiled. "Then we don't have to marry right now."

I hesitated. "When did you have in mind?"

"Valentine's Day."

"But that's less than two months!"

He shook his head. "The following year. That gives you over a year to adjust to our new partnership before we take the plunge."

"You'd wait that long?"

"Some things are worth waiting for. Besides, it's not as if we won't be together."

"Why Valentine's Day? I didn't know you were a romantic."

"I'm not." The mischief I loved so well twinkled in his blue eyes. "I figured it would help me remember our anniversary."

I took a deep breath and held out my left hand.

"Is that a *yes?*" he asked.

With my throat too tight with emotion to speak, I nodded and he slid the ring on my finger. I held up my hand to the light and the aquamarines sparkled like the sunlight on the waters of the Gulf, as deep and enduring as my love for him.

The sound of church bells, pealing midnight with a joyful clamor, carried through the open door.

"A good omen," Bill said.

"A good omen," I agreed.

I snuggled deeper into his embrace and lifted my face to his kiss.

* * * * *

Don't miss the continuing relationship of Maggie and Bill—both professionally and personally—when Charlotte Douglas's next Harlequin NEXT book, SPRING BREAK, comes out in April 2006!

The colder the winter, the sweeter the blackberries will be once spring arrives.

Will the Kimball women discover the promise of a beautiful spring?

Blackberry WINTER

Cheryl REAVIS

A bear ate my ex, and that's okay.

Stacy Kavanaugh is convinced
that her ex's recent disappearance
in the mountains is the worst
thing that can happen to her.
In the next two weeks, she'll
discover how wrong she really is!

Grin and Bear It
Leslie LaFoy

Kate Austin makes
a captivating debut
in this luminous tale
of an unconventional
road trip…and one
woman's metamorphosis.

dragonflies AND dinosaurs

KATE AUSTIN

REQUEST YOUR
FREE BOOKS!

2 FREE NOVELS
TO INTRODUCE
YOU TO OUR
BRAND-NEW LINE!

There's the life you planned. And there's what comes next.

Three friends,
two exes
and a plan
to get payback.

The Payback Club
by Rexanne Becnel
USA TODAY BESTSELLING AUTHOR

A woman determined to walk her own path

Joining a gym was the last thing Janine ever expected to do. But with each step on that treadmill, a new world of possibilities was opening up!

TREADING LIGHTLY
ELISE LANIER

HN28TALL

Available January 2006
TheNextNovel.com